Evil Eye
and Other Stories

NATACHA STEWART

Evil Eye
and Other Stories

1972

HOUGHTON MIFFLIN COMPANY BOSTON

With the exception of "Evil Eye,"
all the stories in this book appeared
originally in *The New Yorker*.

First Printing c

for William Maxwell

Contents

Evil Eye
and Other Stories

Evil Eye

"WE HAVEN'T REALLY been introduced, you know," the
woman said in a loud voice that shook with the vibra-
tions of the boat.

She spoke very slowly, very clearly.

"I'm from Capetown. My name is Theodora White, and
I teach biology."

It was hard to know whether or not she was serious. After
a silent recess, she said with finality: "You may call me
Theodora."

"I'm Larry," said the boy.

He did not get up because the boat, or caïque, to be more
exact, had begun to roll very badly; but he bowed slightly
from the waist, for he was an old-fashioned boy, who went
to an old-fashioned school.

"Lawrence?" Theodora asked. "The laurel? Splendid
name for Delos. I shall call you Lawrence. Sacred to Apollo.
Couldn't be more perfect, although perfection, as you know,
is an end in itself. Inspired both poetry and prophecy —
Lawrence, I mean. Ever heard of a poet laureate?"

(All this in a quaking contralto.)

She watched him steadily, gray eyes wide apart, until, all of a sudden, she had to placate her straw hat to her head with her right hand. Her left, meantime, kept a French *Guide Bleu* (Grèce) firmly anchored to her lap. It was open to "Ile de Délos" (text to the left, detailed map to the right). The narrow ribbon marker, striped yellow, green, and red, flew in the wind. With ambidextrous precision, she drew it back into its line of duty, shut the book, and deposited it to her left, on the varnished planks that rimmed the whole inside of the caïque. Thus liberated, she sighed and crossed her right leg over her left, worn navy blue sneaker over worn navy blue sneaker, the right one laced with a brand-new, bright red shoelace.

Larry watched her as she straightened her back and stretched, legato, until, subito, she had to bring her left arm to the rescue of her right. She made it. And now, out of relief, and, no doubt, innate kindness, tattered straw hat finally secured by amphora-shaped arms, she smiled at Larry.

It was an ineffably sad and brownish smile, and the boy thought: Either they are short of dentists in Capetown (overly committed to heart transplants), or else this is the result of a defective diet when she was young.

There was no doubt that Larry was overly conscious of teeth. For some unexplainable reason, except, perhaps, the miscalculations of *two* orthodontists, he was still in braces at the age of sixteen. This business had gone on forever, it seemed. It was pitiful, relentless, and grotesque. Every one of his teeth was sheathed in metal, and semicircular hands ringed both the upper and lower jaws. When he yawned, and forgot to put his hand in front of his mouth, the sight was, according to his mother, "more sadomasochistic kitchen Cellini than healthy young lion at the zoo." He *hated* it when his mother thought she was being clever. She only succeeded in being cruel, and he was an only child.

And when he slept, he had to wear something called a "neckpiece." It was very close to an instrument of·torture, and he suffered terribly.

Emotionally, it more or less paralyzed him. The humiliation of it all; and no end in sight, no understanding from his parents. It was as if they had grown tired of understanding. But did parents ever understand in the first place? *Could* they understand? *Really* understand? He thought not.

His mother, at irregular intervals, would look at him sideways (God, how he knew that look) and then call his father into the room, and his father would close the door behind him, and they would have an animated exchange. (Of course Larry, as soon as he saw the *look*, left the room as fast as he could and waited until he heard the door open.)

And once it did open, he always felt tracked down, pinned to the wall, looked at through a newly invented microscope that had never been used before. It was the bills, of course. As if he were the cause of it all; as if it were his fault. They never seemed to think that he had enough troubles of his own. Such as what he was going to do when he grew up. He wanted to be a writer. His literature teacher summarily noted in the margin of one of his trimestrial reports: "Writes beautifully." And he did.

But what was he going to do right now? An hour from now? Look at broken columns. But beyond that? There always seemed to be a beyond these days, as if the present was overfull, yet incomplete, and failed to take care of itself.

He would look down, overnight, and discover that his

trousers no longer fitted him. But had he looked down for the past three weeks? *Really* looked? That very morning, he had noticed that his jeans had moved up to an unpresentable length; it was hard to say, looking down; but definitely three or two inches above the ankle-bone.

". . . like an asparagus . . ." His mother had said contentedly when he had come home at the end of the school year.

And it was true that he grew like those flowers and plants and ferns he had seen in a revival of a French film a few weeks ago; with time solidly compressed and the camera held completely still, so that the plant stretched in front of your eyes; grew and grew until it simply *had* to bloom or unfurl its leaves without any gentleness at all — with an irrevocable violence, as if it had no choice at all. What *was* the name of that film? He could not remember. He was going gaga, like his maternal grandmother before she died. (Tinkly music on the soundtrack; probably Vivaldi; even more probably *The Seasons*.) And still he could not remember the name of the film. Power failure; as if at times there was not enough psychic energy left for both retentive memory and physical expansion. (Or was it the sun, the sea, the recent life he led?) He just hoped he would soon be rewired correctly, and by that he did not mean the braces on his teeth.

There were too many things he could not talk about, except to a psychologist, perhaps. He wondered whether or not a psychologist would be able to get him to talk. It most certainly would take him a long time. His friend Terence went to a psychologist because he stuttered. Terence still stuttered but he did say that he had learned to like to talk; it was such a relief to talk to someone who simply had to listen and was not a parent.

Larry yawned in the wind. In the middle of the yawn he remembered to put his hand in front of his mouth (". . . please, Larry dear; all that scrap iron . . ." — his mother again). He stretched his legs. Nothing much on the horizon. In his angle of vision, the island, like the attenuated back of a hippo, protruded from the sea, which was rough. The caïque rolled; the sound of its motor precluded conversation. He would speak only if spoken to. He would certainly not volunteer. He stretched again.

And again. There was no one around to tell him not to. Theodora appeared to be kind and easy. Perhaps she taught sixteen-year-olds.

II

On the job, he could no longer stretch. Madame Duperrex had allowed herself to tell him this was conduct unbefitting a tutor. "Even an illegal tutor?" Larry had wanted to ask, but did not. Madame Duperrex would have said the same to one of her own sons, etc., etc., etc.

"I am a contraband tutor in a police state." This was Larry's silent refrain of the summer. He had made it: the Greek island of his London dreams. He felt all set, full-blown, grown-up, and vastly responsible. He turned slightly toward Theodora and stretched again, his hands clasped above his head.

He did not like his job but loved his month in Greece. No real pay, but a round-trip airplane ticket — London-Athens, and the other way around. Room, board, and pocket money at the employer's discretion. The employer was discreet, the bed was like a board, and the board did strange things to his stomach at first. It was unlike anything he had ever eaten before, but there was plenty of it and nobody complained when he went into the refrigerator, which was about every three hours except when sound asleep or at the table.

His father had told him he would learn, at long last, the value of money. His mother had told him not to hesitate to telephone if something dreadful happened. (She obviously had no previous experience with Greek telephones.) But Larry felt fully protected; it was a happy arrangement.

Madame Duperrex was very precise. Monsieur Duperrex was kind. He liked to putter around with flashlights and lanterns, which was helpful, because when they had first arrived, the approach to the house, from the narrow dirt path soiled with goat, donkey, and human excrement, past the squeeky wooden door, down the steep and curving steps covered in prickly pears that fell from giant cacti, to the house itself that was built on three levels, had been illuminated by nothing more reliable than the light of the moon.

The house stood in the middle of nowhere: far enough from the village to make shopping difficult, and far enough from any of the beaches to necessitate taking a bus.

It was a nice little house that relied heavily on charm. Its owner, a French professor who taught mathematics at Columbia, and his wife ("*joli talent d'artiste-peintre*," according to Madame Duperrex, who had known her, as a child) had decided to resist the colonels by dividing their summer between Riverside Drive and Fire Island; a silent and honest, although doomed to remain anonymous, enough protest. Madame Duperrex had also hinted that her vague old friend might be short of cash, and that it had always been her own dream to see Greece, colonels or no colonels. "All that old culture," she had repeated many many times. She was bitterly disappointed.

She must have had her boys quite late in life, because she belonged to that particular generation of women who cannot walk barefoot or in flat shoes and who wear mules with their dressing gowns. And she had no night vision whatsoever, which, of course, could happen to anyone, but it was a struggle to get her out of the house after sundown. Nor could she reconcile herself to the very primitive kitchen or the arid, spiky, almost abstract garden — a rarity on the island — that surrounded the house and released mosquitoes at nightfall instead of perfume. Between all this and the local wind that blew incessantly and whose name she could never remember, Madame Duperrex was totally lost.

The two boys, aged fourteen and twelve, were real dunces. Larry's job was to teach them English — if possible, within August's thirty-one days. Madame Duperrex had somehow arrived at the conclusion that, without English today, no one could get anywhere, not even the French in France. This was a new and revolutionary theory (for Madame Duperrex) and she was very pleased with herself for having put it into practice.

Larry taught the boys with homemade cards and simple dialogue, a method he had chosen the moment he had been hired through the mails: "I enclose a photo taken of me two weeks ago exactly . . ." (hopefully anticipating a new passport). He had tried to sound organized, which his father, often enough, had told him he was not. He had apparently succeeded. Madame Duperrex screamed at her sons in a high-pitched voice. Larry could not tell where she came from, originally. (The Limousin.) His French was improving.

"Jean-Marc et Daniel-Georges!" This was the theme that ran through all of their days. Jean-Marc was the younger of the two, but they were both impossible, and she was right to scream. She never screamed at Larry. Because he was very careful, for one thing. He took a chance with the refrigerator, but that seemed to be all right.

And Madame Duperrex never screamed at the maid, who had come with the house automatically, like a sole and formidable fair-weather figure in a barometer. (For it was always fair weather.) The maid did all the beds because the boys wouldn't even do these. She swept the dust and sand out with an old and ragged broom. She washed clothes, bent in two over a cloud cover of foam in the only bathtub in the house. This she seemed to like. She used far too much water, which by August had become very scarce on the island, but Madame Duperrex was so terrified of her that she didn't dare say anything. Besides, she couldn't. The maid worked barefoot; she left her sandals ceremoniously outside the kitchen door, as if she were about to enter a mosque. Nobody knew her name. She was sullen, mustachioed, and strong. She communicated in slow pantomime. Madame Duperrex left her strictly alone; all she did was throw the wash in the tub for her. That message was clear enough. After all, the maid might disappear and never appear again the next morning. Who knew where she lived? She wanted no lunch, which was good. And when she left, Madame Duperrex' ample pink underpants and wired bra, pinned on the line next to Monsieur Duperrex' conservative shorts, flew in the wind like twin domestic banners against the Aegean sky and one cypress tree.

The more serious washing the maid took away with her wrapped in a neat bundle, a sheet with its four corners knotted, which she wore over her arm like a basket. Madame Duperrex never knew whether or not she would ever see it again. Nor could she pick up a single word of Greek; her learning powers were at a total standstill. And the maid had an infuriating habit; in answer to Madame Duperrex' pantomime, she moved her head slowly from side to side, which in Greek, meant "yes." Up and down meant "no." And

Madame Duperrex couldn't catch on. She was too busy —
Larry's deduction — with the dust and dirt and small stones
that entered her open shoes with medium heels; with the
passage of donkeys in the narrow streets of the village and
what they left behind; with the amount of olive oil in her
plate (natural enough); and the absence of deck chairs on
the beach (more recherché). Larry was hypnotized by
the unexpected number of jars of cream busily aligned on
the marble top of the chest of drawers in her bedroom. His
mother had only one and washed her face with glycerine
soap. But this was incredible. Small and large, fat and
tall, all round, all pink, sometimes stacked one on top of
the other, ready to attack. (Agincourt!) Attack what?
Wrinkles and a double chin, and general dissatisfaction
with her life and with her sons. That one was easy. What
Larry couldn't make out was the way she felt, or didn't
feel, about Monsieur Duperrex.

Jean-Marc and Daniel-Georges, spread out in pajamas
on their unmade bunks at ten A.M., the exact hour when
Larry's lesson was supposed to begin. They read *Astérix*
and *Lucky Luke* and *Le Journal de Tintin* and *Spirou* and
Pilote.

"Daniel-Georges et Jean-Marc!"

Now they are being called to order. A lot that would do.
Daniel-Georges had lost an irreplaceable English grammar
and by the time another one arrived, they would all be
gone, and that included, perhaps and hopefully, even the
colonels. That's how efficient the mails were. Meanwhile,
homework was very vague, because the boys said they
couldn't work out of the same grammar without cheating.

As for Jean-Marc, he dropped the skins of figs wherever
he happened to stand and eat them. His narrow desk drawers
were filled with the shells of pistachio nuts and the fossils

from bunches of grapes. Also the pips. (In that way, he was very tidy.) And he had a cache of sweet sesame bars; he chewed on them whenever his parents weren't about and even offered some to Larry, who couldn't touch them because of his braces — worse than nougat. When Jean-Marc finished a sesame bar, he hid the sticky-sweet, transparent wrapping among his clean underwear. It was true that his mother had lately complained about his lack of appetite, but Jean-Marc couldn't stop. He ran the convoluted streets of the village, following the voice of the old man with the large stain of sweat under the armpits of his otherwise immaculate white shirt, the voice that shouted, "Se*sa*me, Se*sa*me," with the accent on the second syllable. Larry kept a mature silence, although he had told Jean-Marc firmly, in private, to get off the candy bars. This, somehow, more than anything else had made him feel adult and in charge of his charges.

His own parents had been delighted with his idea of an independent summer, and had helped him toward it. But of course the future reality is never what you expect it to be while stuck in the irremediable past. Not that he missed his parents, but he was pleased to have them, in an abstract sort of way. He wondered how he would feel about that particular month of August, once it was past. Imagine what it would be like to have been born into the Duperrex family: Daniel-Georges' and Jean-Marc's elder brother. Larry shivered in the wind.

"Put on your sweater!" Theodora half shouted. "Right, right," Larry mumbled. It was tied by the sleeves around his waist. He pulled it on.

So — he had escaped Madame Duperrex, his foster mother, for the end of an afternoon, only to fall into the hands and under the orders of a third. This one, however, delighted him, she was so outrageous.

The wind rose, as unexpectedly as if a door had opened to a violent draft, and the sailor rushed out of his deckhouse. He gripped the worn planks of the open deck with enormous bare feet. The caïque was much too large for him to handle alone, and he appeared to be in a panic. Larry, by now, was on to the fact that a Greek never kept calm, so he tried not to worry. The roll did not bother him; it was the lurch he feared. Now the sailor rushed in and out of the tiny deckhouse. Each time, he had to leave the door loose and free to bang. He left the wheel unattended in order to deal with the line. Then he rushed in again and closed the door. Delos was still quite far off. The muted light was forever confusing distances. The trip took longer than it should have — they had been underway for twenty-five minutes — and Delos still looked like the back of a half-immersed hippo. But the outline had become clear; now only the distance and the untrue light kept it a dark, deep gray.

The boat rolled. Larry watched Delos for a moment, afloat, suspended between rough blue water and an impeccably blue sky.

The sailor — whose name was Karalombo — had greeted them on board with an enormous smile that had shown off several expensive gold teeth. That, added to the facts that he had obviously been a sailor all his life and that Theodora was peacefully absorbed in a daydream, reassured Larry, who was thinking that he had seen nothing yet that could even approach the idea of a "wine-dark" sea. He looked out again. He dared only look forward, toward the prow of the boat. To look back was forbidden, at that particular moment in time. Before he could look back, something had to happen: the sound of a voice, a movement, a cry.

So Larry looked toward Delos. The sea was blue. Not cobalt, not sapphire, not lapis-lazuli (Larry liked minerals and stones), but blue, in a way that only the sea can be blue.

He thought he might ask Theodora about that elusive "wine-dark" sea but the sound of the engine stopped him. Also, she was now totally absorbed in her daydream. She threw the butt of her cigarette overboard, like a ritual pinch of salt, over her left shoulder. She almost hit him in the face with it.

III

Theodora. The Duperrex. He had forgotten about them for a few minutes. They must be nouveaux riches. Parvenus. Arrivistes. There was no doubt that his French was improving, even if Daniel-Georges' and Jean-Marc's English remained more or less static. Deceptive about Monsieur Duperrex. He had something to do with French roads. The boys boasted a lot and Larry did not know what to believe — especially because they were on an island where sun and sky and sand and sea and one's own enjoyment and food were the only commodities (together with the mustachioed maid), where there were no cars, only one main road, no occasion or possibility to show off furniture, paintings, art, jewels or furs. It was deceptive about Monsieur Duperrex, if indeed he had all the money the boys boasted about. He probably dealt in all kinds of different enterprises. "Never ask where the first million comes from" (Larry's mother, overheard). A million what? Francs? Dollars? Who cared? Certainly not Larry. And Monsieur Duperrex seemed to be so mild a man. But you never knew. He might be what Larry's father called, following a trip to the United States, "a shark in business." Any important animals in the Aegean Sea? He would ask Theodora later.

Theodora. Paired off with Theodora on a trip to Delos. The illicit tutor of sixteen and the teacher of biology well into her fifties. It was difficult to tell her exact age, because she had something called "spirit" and no gray in her hair. Paired off with Theodora, for a hopelessly chaste afternoon among the ruins.

Tessa. What of Tessa? Where *was* Tessa? Larry looked at his watch. He had managed, for a prodigious twenty-eight minutes, not to keep her constantly at the back of his mind. She was there and he knew that she was there, but he had not brooded over her incessantly. He had held his head toward Theodora and Delos and forced himself not to look back, and had succeeded. A victory for him, because he had been under Tessa's spell since the second of August.

IV

Actually, Tessa was right at the stern, in the same caïque. Larry heard her laugh, and then he heard Marco laugh. They laughed together. Larry lowered his eyes. Tessa had stared at him as he had climbed aboard, a sustained stare, and then her stare had taken in Theodora, and Tessa had smiled — the first time she had ever smiled at him. And that smile had made him want, while he stepped aboard very carefully, for fear of a stubbed toe, to throw himself into the Aegean Sea and drown (painlessly, if possible, without the three stabs of memory. They would all, at that moment, have included Tessa, like three consecutive scenes in the same reel of film).

Beloved Tessa.

Marco.

The Italians.

Marco.

Larry had seen Marco board the bus at the crossroads,

not far from the Duperrex house, between the village and the beach. Marco stood barefoot in the dust; he walked back and forth, for he could never stand still. He wore sparse black bathing trunks and nothing else, except for a large, flat, engraved silver Moroccan hand hung on a heavy silver chain. The chain was long and the Moroccan hand almost reached his navel. Sometimes he reversed it and let the hand pat him rhythmically on the back as he paced. In any case, he would board that overcrowded bus. (Sometimes the doors wouldn't close; Larry had never known anything like it. The tube in London had never been like that, not even at rush hour.) And sometimes Marco rode barefoot on the lower step of the back door, vulnerable because of his nakedness and yet tough, with his four-drachma fare in hand. How did he get back? Did he borrow? Did he bum? It seemed as if Marco could not think further than the action he was momentarily engaged in; it was as if he could not think beyond stepping onto the bus in order to get to the beach. He got off (and so did Larry) at this summer's fashionable beach.

They all did. The Italians, and the few token Greeks, and the Duperrex family. At the beach, Marco never stood or sat or lay still for more than a few seconds. Mostly he roamed, Moroccan hand in hand. He dropped it only to comb his long, partless hair with his fingers. Then he picked up his third hand again. Then he spoke to a girl, but did not stop long enough to even turn his head toward her. Then roamed up to another, lay down beside a third, only to get up because now there was sand in his hair. So he threw himself headfirst into the sea, disappeared, and surfaced again, face to the beach, and stumbled out with a grimace because of the stones on the sharply sloped bottom.

Dearest Tessa.

Quickly, Larry looked back at Theodora.

v

He had met Theodora that very morning under a thatched umbrella at the beach. Madame Duperrex, in an off moment, had given him the rest of the day off. It was then almost eleven o'clock, and he had begun work at six. He had gone down to the village for provisions and come up again with a basket that weighed a ton. (Wine, beer, olives, cheese without holes in it, a can of olive oil, etc.) He had had to change hands regularly on the way up and had taken a moment off to stretch his arms above his head. Nor had he forgotten the yogurt (four containers), which Madame Duperrex favored. It could only be obtained from a single store on the docks, which prolonged the shopping expedition by forty minutes at least.

He had daydreamed (Tessa mostly, with the interruption of a projected dialogue with Terence) through part of his own lesson: "The sun is bright; the bus goes to the beach; the sea is very cold; the sun; I repeat: the *sun* . . ."

And then, Madame Duperrex, very quietly, had walked into the sun-dappled room and interrupted the three of them: Jean-Marc with his eyes three-quarters closed, his head in his arms, and his arms crossed on the rickety wooden table; Daniel-Georges concentratedly picking his nose; and Larry simultaneously reciting and watching two flies about to . . . copulate. (No, flies did not copulate; they did not make love either. Did they mate? What *did* they do? Lions, he was certain, made love.)

"The sand is hot, extremely hot," said Larry.

Madame Duperrex stood in the doorway. She leaned toward the handle of the door she had just opened, called her boys to attention.

"Jean-Marc et Daniel-Georges!"

And suddenly told Larry he could go for the rest of the day. It was his first time off in three weeks. He grazed past Madame Duperrex with a light murmur of "Merci, merci," ran into the bathroom, snatched the first, none too clean bath towel that lay on the floor, collected the change on the dresser in his bedroom, pulled a shirt from a drawer that never closed and his sandals from under the bed, straightened out, ran through the open door, and climbed the stone steps of the garden with a pounding heart, terrified at the last-minute possibility of Madame Duperrex' voice, imperious and regretful, calling him back.

"Lar*ry*."

But she did not.

VI

Larry had gone to the beach the Duperrex dragged him to daily. He had neither the time nor the energy to strike out for either the new or the nudist. He did want to see the nudist beach. They had almost gone, once. Monsieur Duperrex had asked his wife to accompany him, but she said that they would have to take a taxi, and the boys, *and* Larry, and that she would look awfully stupid "avec mon derrière tout blanc," a phrase which Larry found unbelievably vulgar, perhaps because Madame Duperrex' derrière could not so easily be dismissed.

He knew that Tessa would be at their daily beach. Tessa, unless sick or gone, or trampled to death while trying to get on or off the bus, would be there. She came every day. Tessa, and the others.

Larry called her immediate circle "the Italians." Tessa, and Francesco. Francesco was very important. And Marco. And Marisa. And Sandro.

And, of course, Tessa's mother and father. And then there was a Greek girl who moved in and out of the magic circle and looked as if she had detached herself from a wall off the palace at Knossos. She was sixteen, perhaps seventeen. They were all young. Marco was about nineteen. Francesco was older, in his early twenties, but tired-looking, which might have added a year or two.

Most of the crowd on the beach was young and carefree, either silenced and dazed by sun or sea, or else very noisy. They all laughed with their heads thrown back, something Larry did not know how to do. And he belonged to no one, particularly when he came with the Duperrex.

Everybody else seemed to be part of a larger design: a small group was a square; a pair looked like a narrow rectangle. The Italians formed a circle. They danced in the round, unless the wind blew with the force of a gale, and then they took refuge on a tiled terrace that extended from the restaurant on the beach; it was protected from the wind by a low stone wall. Larry called it "the Italian Enclosure."

It was a summer of innocence (if you could call Madame Duperrex innocent) played out against a backdrop of unknown anguish and continual surprise.

The young Greek who owned the restaurant on the beach (married to an English girl and father of a four-year-old terror named Sam, probably the world's most accomplished demolisher of sand castles) had just been heavily fined by the police for wearing his hair too long. This morning, he had looked unfamiliar, mutilated even, after a hasty, military-looking haircut.

Larry gathered information slowly. The most popular composer in Greece was banned. But a certain singer, in a certain nightclub, sang the forbidden songs, vibrato, late at night (eyes closed, head back) when the crowds had gone and he could trust the few remaining faces.

A bomb had lately exploded in Athens; in the middle of Constitution Square. But didn't bombs explode everywhere? It was like suicide, or divorce, for that matter. So many countries seemed to compete for the highest rate.

The word "tyrant" was banned. So was the word "sin." A nightclub called Seven Sins had been officially reduced to a geographically vague "Seven Seas." The sins had been easy, even for Jean-Marc. But the newly disembarked tourist always wanted to know which were the Seven Seas. Nobody bothered, and he was usually told, "Meet you at the Seven Sins at nine." At nine, the crowd was so dense in the narrow street that it blocked the entrance to the club. It was the popular rendezvous of the island.

The Italians were always there; they usually linked on to another part of a human chain and filed out to the docks for a late dinner.

VII

Slowly, Larry added up the facts, and they added up to very little.

One evening, during the first week in August, they all had dinner at the docks. All the tourists ate at the tavernas quite late. It was so much easier than eating at home, more fun than eating at a hotel, and cheaper than either.

The four Duperrex and Larry had just come from the kitchen of the taverna, where they had looked at all the food and then chosen what they were going to eat.

It was delightful to be allowed to take the covers off the big pots on the stoves, inhale the sage and the basil, observe the perfect oval of enormous white beans, and then, in a special spot just off the kitchen, see the cold foods laid out in the dining room itself with all the poetic exactitude of a still life. The almost one-dimensional fish, its mouth open and its white scales veined like marble in pinky red; the pastel vegetable salads held under glass, or left to the direct glaze of neon lights. (Larry liked paper-thin cucumber and yogurt best.)

It was almost impossible to choose, everything looked so delicious. And so very cheap too, according to Madame Duperrex. She never held back the boys. She let them have an occasional beer and generally devour everything in sight like wolves. Most of the time, she watched them contentedly; only once in a great while, her shaken feminine sensibilities would force her to tell them to calm down and eat like human beings.

The wind had died down and so they ate at a round table outside. It was covered with a plastic tablecloth printed with token flowers. Anything made out of plastic was considered a luxury on the island. They were served by a pale child with long braids, pierced ears, eyes like black cherries, and the wisdom of the ages already stamped on the delicate lines of her cheeks.

The docks were crowded. Every table in every taverna was occupied. It was nine o'clock in the evening. Tattered young men in beards walked by quickly, entwined with barefoot girls. Older men, mostly Greek, walked more slowly, hand in hand with their women.

They had mixed sufflaki (shish kebab, with onions, peppers, and tomatoes). There was a momentary silence as they chewed the fresh, rather tough lamb. Then, suddenly, Monsieur Duperrex said quite emphatically: "See this man? He's an informer."

Larry looked up quickly from his plate. He saw a tall man, young and strong, with each of his arms around a different girl. The man said something and the three of them laughed. The girls leaned heavily against him. The man was tall for a Greek. He wore the sailor's cap that was the uniform of most of the men on the island, which the tourists could buy at the docks; dark trousers; and a white T-shirt with the letters c.c.n.y. solidly blocked across the chest. The man laughed aloud, quite loud, gaily, and walked on. He appeared to be amiable enough.

Then Monsieur Duperrex said: "Last year they had an American beach bum in their pay. A charming young man, from what I've been told. But he was paid to spy on the tourists, and report on what he saw and heard. He slept on the sand, under the stars."

Larry felt rather strange. He was totally apolitical, and he did not quite know what he should think. A prolonged silence, while they all ate, until Monsieur Duperrex broke it to say: "They arrest people of the extreme left at dusk." (Monsieur Duperrex appeared to speak from the depths of an unusually poetical mood. Actually, the sentence sounded much better in French: "Ils arrêtent les gens d'extrême-gauche au crépuscule."

It was a difficult sentence, and Larry had to pause, fork in hand, think, and translate it for himself. Was dusk the classical time for arrests? He had always thought it to be dawn.

They ordered dessert: baklava, a thousand-layered puff-pastry generously interlined with honey. Madame Duperrex abstained with that fleeting, ghostlike expression that often passes over the face of women who love to eat but know they must diet and are being watched. She ordered yogurt instead. Baklava was, at the moment, Larry's very favorite food — more than a delight, a sort of adolescent Turkish rapture.

At that point, Monsieur Duperrex dove into the horrors

of prison and several forms of torture. Brutal beatings, especially on the soles of the feet, had the advantage of leaving little or no traces. Monsieur Duperrex, his baklava untouched, seemed to want to spare nothing and no one.

"Electrodes?" asked Jean-Marc, his eyes open wide, his mouth full, a drop of honey stuck to his chin and illuminated by a street lamp near the water.

"Jean-Marc!" (A call to order — Madame Duperrex.)

Monsieur Duperrex, also silenced, attacked his baklava. Larry finished his and looked up, then left and right and all around. The Italians, that night, were nowhere in sight.

Madame Duperrex finally said to her husband, "You have cut the children's appetites."

Larry looked around the table. Everyone had finished except for Madame Duperrex, who with a pointy spoon still scraped the last, left-over ridges of yogurt from her tilted plastic container.

The informer had completely disappeared, gone to dance, probably, in a taverna.

It was all very unreal.

VIII

That summer, there was only one type of matchbox for sale on the island — an ordinary, wooden matchbox with the junta's symbol on it, a dead black, sharp silhouette of a sentry with helmet, rifle, and bayonet against a background of hellish orangy red flames that rose to transform themselves into the yellow wings and head of the ever-useful phoenix. Above the phoenix' head it said GREECE in Greek, and under the soldier's feet, APRIL 21ST.

Madame Duperrex chain-smoked, forever misplacing her matches and never displacing herself unless it was abso-

lutely necessary, so Larry quickly learned to spot the sol-
dier-in-the-flames. He had smoked only two cigarettes in
three weeks; how his mother would be pleased if she knew.
In any case, he did not even want to smoke: it was a sin to
mar, in any way, that honey-sweet sea air.

The Greeks on the island looked happy. Larry, indiscriminately, felt that he liked everyone he met.

That August was, for him, a month of sudden emotional
exchange. Outside of his feelings for the Duperrex family,
which were too complicated to analyze — he did not have
the time — it was a month of love.

Three days after his arrival, he burst the zipper on his jeans
and had to take them to a tailor. With pantomime and one
Greek word ("please"), he had explained to the stooped
man in steel-rimmed glasses that he had only two pairs of
long trousers and he needed his jeans back as soon as possible. Whereupon the tailor had looked at him attentively,
risen from his chair, and, across the narrow table with the
sewing machine in a timeless and placeless gesture of love,
taken Larry into his arms, murmuring a long string of incomprehensible words that must have meant reassurance
and encouragement into the boy's right ear. When the tailor
released him, he felt on the verge of tears, which was unusual except for the fact that he had come alone to a strange
country, and had just been caught off guard. Slightly abashed,
Larry gave in return his only other word of Greek ("thank
you"). When he returned toward evening, he knew three
more words ("good morning"; "good afternoon"; "good
evening").

"Good afternoon," said Larry to the tailor, who gave him
an enormous smile almost evenly divided between enamel
and gold. As for his jeans, they were neatly pressed and laid
out over the back of a chair next to the one the tailor sat on.

The zipper had been replaced and the price charged so ephemeral that Larry blushed.

The regime operated behind the scenes and the people Larry met lived outside it, for the most part, because the island was, in that month of August, first and foremost a very crowded tourist resort.

The wind, transforming several of the narrow streets that issued onto the docks into wind tunnels which were difficult to get through, often took Larry's breath away. Still, he loved the island so much that in spite of the colonels, who necessarily remained a political abstraction to him, he already planned to build himself a simple, white-washed house, preferably on a rock, somewhere in the dry wilderness marked only by a miraculous number of consecrated one-room churches, each with a cross and a red roof. In this way, he would be able to escape from the rigors of his future life.

He had planned it all through part of a sleepless, mosquito-riddled night. The house, and how he would make it easily accessible from the port and the village — and to the beaches, with the help of a Harley-Davidson.

IX

Meanwhile, he was reconciled to being a tourist among tourists, and earning his keep besides. Carefully, he watched the life around him; the islanders complained, mostly about the wind, in order to please tourists. And the tourists complained about the meltémi, because tourists always complain. The meltémi was to Greece what the mistral is to southern France, the foehn to the Alps, and the sirocco to North Africa.

That summer, the tourists had a right to say that they swallowed dust on the roads, sand with their watermelon, and sand nature when they lay on the beaches. Dust and sand clung to their throats, their nostrils, their hair, their ears, and their eyelashes. Both men and women wore enormous sunglasses, that summer's fashion, more against wind than sun. They said the meltémi seriously interfered with their holiday mood (whatever that was) and their concentration on paperbound novels. It was perfectly true that the books did take off while the reader turned, on the beach, from one elbow to the other. And newspapers flew off like kites if you just sneezed and forgot, for a split second, to hold on with all your might and landed peacefully, somewhere out at sea.

Having returned from the beaches and gone on to shop and explore (trailed by *bouzouki* music), the tourists complained of getting lost.

There were two theories about the whitewashed, labyrinthian village: 1) that it had been built specifically in order to confuse pirates; 2) that it had been built solely in order to confuse the wind.

Both theories were valid. At least one was correct and either one was still applicable.

The contemporary pirate, who masquerades as a tourist (one-way sunglasses instead of an eye patch; Instamatic camera substituting for a telescope), had to ask the way at every street corner — although his eventual destination might have been as foolproof as the docks, and so was instantly recognized as an intruder, in spite of the fact that he was camouflaged to begin with: his eyes (behind the one-way sunglasses) riveted to a large, unfolded map of the island that he carried delicately, like an immense open book, a feat in itself because the map at times exceeded the width of a street. And then, of course, there was the wind . . .

On blowy days, all the streets that opened onto the port

became wind tunnels. As a counterpoint, once lost inside the village, the tourist came upon unexpected squares that were like individual womb-islands of total peace — where a barren fig tree in a corner hardly breathed; where an outdoor restaurant, covered by an awning that did not even flap, became a dark pool of shade; where the revolutions of a suckling pig on its spit had been momentarily arrested as the waiter daydreamed, long-ashed cigarette in hand, elbows on a flowered plastic tablecloth, eyes slowly blinking to the blare of the *bouzouki* he never thought of turning off.

Larry learned a few more facts, very few, about the islands in general.

Most of the women seemed to be called Sofia.

Most of the hotels were called Xenia. Was it a chain of hotels, like the Hiltons? Or did the word "Xenia" have a special meaning? He did not know but intended to find out.

One thing, for Larry, who usually vacationed with his parents on the Isle of Wight, remained totally magical. It never rained. Every night before he went to sleep, Larry rocked himself with the repeated words, "It won't rain tomorrow." And every morning, he was awakened shortly, at dawn just before five, by the same subdued, but already apricot-warm light of day.

The Greek men on the island had great presence, wide smiles, and enormous hands and feet. They sang a lot. At night, they danced in the tavernas (heavy sweat, deep pliés, and a waving handkerchief).

The women were almost unbearably kind. If Larry lost his way in the winding streets, they escorted him back where he belonged, no matter how far he had strayed, each one with a ball of wool under her left armpit, knitting all the while.

They could never put their work down, because the thread of the wool ingeniously ran through a safety pin fastened just under their left shoulder. Ariadnes, all of them. Ariadnes of all shapes and ages.

And through the days and through the nights the *bouzouki* blared: from the buses, from any one of the four taxis parked at the docks, from every taverna, from the lounge of every ship that ferried or cruised, from the dark of anonymous rooms, open to the narrow streets for air at night. Transistorized and blurred, it rose from the protective shadow of beach towels and bags. Wherever you went, *bouzouki* followed.

While on a hillock above the port the sails of four windmills revolved slowly, slowly, until the wind rose, and then they went faster and faster, with a brittle clacking sound, like the paddle wheels of an unknown race of giant children.

x

The greater part of every day was spent at the beach. The island's edge, like a lace doily's, was looped and rimmed by endless beaches and coves. Most of them were still bare and wild, and almost impossible to get to, except on foot or by boat. The buses rode to the two or three or four beaches that were accessible by road, either paved or dirt.

The Duperrex had been told about a single beach, which turned out to be the fashionable one that summer.

Larry, at first, was terribly disappointed. Instinctively, he had promised himself a warm Mediterranean. He was presented with the Aegean instead. Day after day the wind blew and the water remained bitterly cold. There were no water sports whatsoever. He had hoped to learn to water-ski.

Once, a Zodiac landed on the beach, and a frogman climbed out, all in funereal black except for his face, which was the delicate green of shallow water rimmed by rocks. Larry rushed out to help bring in the boat. The man thanked him. He was English. He removed his diver's knife, which he wore on the inside of his left calf. (Larry was very impressed.) Then he peeled off all of his black rubber second skin, until, stripped to a white triangular bikini, he plunged into the sea once more.

But the next time Larry looked up, he saw the diver back on the beach, wrapped up in a full-length, grass green terry-cloth towel. His teeth chattered. He turned around and hobbled off on geisha-feet to the restaurant for something hot to drink.

The sight was not encouraging.

The men on the beach that summer looked daring and exceedingly vain. Larry, in cut-off blue jeans and faded Lacoste shirt, his outburst of acne penetrated by sun and diminished at last, admired their long hair tangled with salt, their deep caramel skin oiled at regular intervals, their flowered, skin-tight, knee-length, Tahitian bathing trunks. They often wore turn-of-the-century mustaches, beads, charms, and real jewels. The jewelry ranged from leis of seashells and evil-eye charms hung on a suede string to necklaces of amber and silver from Beirut (amber for luck) or a series of fetishes on a long gold chain: a lion's tooth set in gold, a Saint Christopher medal, an Egyptian scarab, a coral hand, a rough turquoise. The possibilities were endless.

The young crowd on the beach spoke French, Spanish, Italian, Greek, English; at times, a little of each all at once. Mostly, they confined themselves to the temperature of the water, the meltémi's daily velocity, a friend's yacht or caïque, and endless inbred gossip.

The girls drooped slightly, pelvises forward, shoulders naturally rounded. They made no attempt either to lift the waist from the pelvis or to hold in their stomach muscles. Their stomachs were beautifully rounded, like on thin Cranachs; their narrow backsides were left to sway in peace. There was no more an attempt at good posture than there would have been from a flower, a cat, or a dragonfly.

The girls were ravishing. They ate enormous quantities of food: moussakas steeped in olive oil, macaroni baked into sweetcakes, rice puddings peppered with cinnamon and crêmes caramel for dessert; after which, with an imperious gesture of the hand, they would summon the barefoot waiter and order a portion of watermelon. A portion was exactly half a watermelon, which dwarfed its plate and arrived, said Daniel-Georges (for once inspired, according to his father), "like a seven forty-seven stuck to a flying saucer." After that, the girls went on to doll-sized cups of Turkish coffee, into which they dropped two lumps of sugar. Given a two- or three-hour pause marked by siestas in the sun and a few dips, they were ready to start all over again. This made Madame Duperrex rightly suspicious. The tone of her voice evenly divided between present jealousy and future revenge, she repeatedly told Monsieur Duperrex over a series of chaste yogurts: "They won't be able to do this when they're older."

But the girls stayed young that summer — dusky, slender, hopelessly young. Sometimes they wore their sunglasses as headbands to keep the long, straight hair out of their eyes, and their naked waists were clasped in thin gold chains which rocked softly with the sunlight as they walked.

*

XI

Larry watched the magic Italian circle and never quite believed what he saw. They looked as if they had been lifted off into an orbit of sunlit beauty that excluded the rest of mankind and had, from time to time, been granted special permission to land. It was inconceivable that they should ever enter an office, face a typewriter, clean a rug, wash a dish, walk along a corridor to a water cooler, address a meeting, fight their way against a high wind on a sooty street, or put the lid on a garbage can.

Their possible itinerary might have read as follows: from the Cyclades, their present stop, to the Seychelles. Then on to Ceylon. Bali. Fiji didn't sound right, but perhaps was. Cozumel. Forgo Round Hill for Anguilla, for the Italians had a true air of exclusive secretiveness about them. Forget Acapulco (too social). To the Azores. Djerba. Hesitate before the Balearic Islands (crowded). Alight, perhaps, in Agrigento for a fleeting week in spring. Porto Ercole, because after all, the entire peninsula of Italy should be granted them as a birthright, for a native playground. Then a short weekend in Corfu, to visit a friend whose health (upper respiratory) had left much to be desired all winter long, and once again the magic circle would be completed, the following summer, with the bare Cyclades.

Larry watched the Italians.

The first one he saw was Tessa, a human cat with improbable eyes: porcelain white and bright cerulean blue. They were huge, inscrutable eyes, heavily underlined and overlined in black or dark blue, depending on her mood and the color of her bikini. Her hair was straight, long, and brown, her walk lazy, and she was lovely beyond belief. She had a

large, perfectly flat mole above her right buttock. But not
really above it — it was on the upper part of her right buttock. That's how brief her bikinis were.

Tessa didn't swim. She went in for dips.

After one of those dips, on the second of August of that
summer, Tessa came out of the water lazily, trailed her hands
behind her over the surface of the water, stubbed something
(must have been a toe, because she stumbled and almost
fell over and swore a loud oath in Italian), after which her
progress over the slanting floor of the sea became even more
careful. She rose slowly, all sleek, almost naked, with stiffened nipples, her darkened skin all in goose pimples and
her hair like dripping drapes. She passed near Larry, who
stood transfixed at the water's edge. He registered a slight,
leftover smell of Coppertone. Then she ran slowly to take
refuge in the Italian Enclosure.

Larry sat down heavily on the wet sand. He was in love.

It was two or three hours later on that same day that
Larry first noticed Francesco, in the restaurant that was
not unlike the inside of a matchbox lying on its side (the
missing partition would have faced the sea).

Larry had told the Duperrex that he would eat on his
own, later. He suddenly felt the need to be alone, to be
away from Jean-Marc and Daniel-Georges, who further
down in the crescent of the beach now fought over the
architecture of their ugly sand castle.

Madame Duperrex had brought along a *Guide Bleu*
(Grèce) that she had found on a bookshelf of the living
room of her rented house.

Wetting her thumb, turning the pages backward, she soon
reached the island of Delos, which, she had been told, was
an absolute *must*.

But then, she had also been told that it was abominably

hot; that she would have to leave at dawn on a creaking
caïque with a picnic; that she would have to listen to a guide
and walk under a relentless sun for hours — all for the
singular privilege of looking at broken columns. *Ruins.* And
that if, by any chance, she wasn't in exactly the right mood,
or the group was not congenial and the light wasn't what it
should be, nothing whatever would happen. (This all came
from the vague childhood friend who had rented her the
house.)

Bravely, Madame Duperrex read on: ". . . Pisistrate,
tyran d'Athènes, purifie le sanctuaire en 543, en le débaras-
sant de ses tombeaux."

Without the slightest interference from a possible, if latent,
sense of obligation, Madame Duperrex decided she would
skip Delos altogether. Of course, if Monsieur Duperrex
wished to go — but no, he wouldn't. Unless she reminded
him.

Wetting her thumb, she turned back a few pages. She
read with satisfaction of the island she had chosen for her
vacation that August, and whose dusty soil she so reluctantly
trod: "(75 km; 3500 hab.), granitique et aride, est devenue de
puis quelques années un grand centre de tourisme."

She wondered, for a moment, why the word "depuis"
was written in two words, but the sun bothered her eyes.

The wind blew. Her concentration was nil. I'm here for
a well-deserved rest, thought Madame Duperrex. So she
shut the book and put it aside, wrapped a black chiffon handkerchief over her eyes, and slowly turned onto her back,
where she now lay like an executed spy, while Monsieur
Duperrex, inevitably, logically, and happily, concentrated
on a Simenon paperback. He had asked not to be disturbed.

Inside the restaurant, Francesco sat with his back against
a wall, his long bare feet on an empty chair. He talked and

talked and talked and talked, without a single interruption, to an older couple, both of whom sat on his right, so that Larry first saw Francesco's head in direct profile. That profile reminded Larry of someone. A second later he knew that the someone was Botticelli's Self-Portrait (detail) from some larger painting in his mother's large book on Botticelli that was covered in pale linen. (His mother was forever trying to give him *culture*. At times, although very rarely, it helped him to understand something; right now, he understood that the young man's looks were not at all contemporary. But where did that get him?)

Francesco's curls were grayed with salt and left uncombed. His profile might have been timeless, but he was dressed with great contemporary care in a high-necked, white shirt embroidered in pale blue, a wide brown leather belt, and brown trousers. He was extremely thin, quite long (even sitting down), and slightly stooped. His right hand alternately fingered and twirled a glass charm against the evil eye on the end of a suede string. Suddenly he laughed, his head thrown back against the flimsy wall, and turned his face to the sea, so that Larry, his stomach all tightened with hunger in spite of the pangs of love as he walked from the restaurant kitchen with moussaka on his plate (cheaper than sufflaki) and a glass of beer, suddenly saw Francesco full face. It was the eyes that stopped him: they were grave, outsize, porcelain white, and cerulean blue.

Larry sat down in the first available chair without asking permission of anyone around the table, as if he had received a slight electric shock, and reached for his beer.

Francesco contained his conversation with the older couple who sat on his right until Tessa crossed the restaurant slowly, twisting and turning in and out of the crowded tables. She had changed into a dry bikini that was the exact shade of her brown skin; she wore leis and leis of seashells that fell below her navel and a fresh white flower in her hair that looked like a tuberose. Larry did not know what those flowers were; only one clump of them grew wild, just beyond the Italian Enclosure.

"Aaaah!" said Francesco very loud, well above the voices around him.

He removed his legs from the empty chair as Tessa came toward him, but instead of taking it, she simply laughed and sat down on his lap. He put his arms around her, and said something into her ear. Tessa buried her face in his neck and covered it in kisses, until Francesco threw her off so that she almost fell. They had a mock fight, and made up when Francesco pulled her to him and kissed her on the forehead. Then Tessa turned to the older couple. She kissed each of them devotedly, on both cheeks. The man's face was hard and furrowed. He had just taken off his glasses and revealed an unmistakable pair of eyes, as startlingly blue and white as Tessa's and Francesco's. Next, Larry looked at the woman. Her loose hair was a dark, striated blond, with lighter, almost white streaks in it. She was still beautiful, but definitely, definitively old (as far as he was concerned), dressed as she was, in a prim, white piqué bikini. She took off and put on her sunglasses all the time, which obviously had a prescription in them. Her eyes were very sad and soft and brown, beginning to film with age like glazed chestnuts. There was no mistake possible; those four were mother, father, daughter, and son.

XII

Over the long days and the short weeks that followed, Larry became obsessed with the Italians. Of course it was Tessa who held him in her spell. But then, so did the others. Marco.

Sandro. Sandro, very dark, still covered in puppy fat, and never without a camera. Marisa, who was Tessa's friend. And the dark girl, who came and went and whose name he never learned.

For one, or two, or three days at a time, new Italians joined the circle; laughter rose; tables were joined together; and then they were gone, as suddenly as they had come.

Larry understood that they were island-hopping, but he did not see the point. This island sufficed for the rest of his life, so long as Tessa was on it.

Tessa and Francesco; her mother and her father. The family was more or less inseparable. Francesco kissed his father on the brow; Tessa walked along the water's edge with her arm wrapped about her mother's waist and whispered in her ear. Tessa rose from her chair, sometimes, to settle in Francesco's lap. Her father tried to throw her into the water once and succeeded, while she screamed for help that never came. In calmer moments, Tessa kissed the palm of her father's hand; Francesco kissed both his mother's cheeks, as he held her lightly by the waist, then rumpled her hair, as she protested and smiled.

Larry envied them their unfeigned gaiety, their unquestionable warmth, the ease with which they laughed and moved and changed their moods. The way Francesco could go to sleep under the sun on the beach, and then rub his eyes like a child when he woke up. The way they ate what they chose, whenever they felt like it. (Sometimes lunch would be close to sundown — five o'clock at that particular beach that August.)

And the reason he envied and loved them was that very abyss that lay between them — those dedicated, pagan people on the beach and his lone self — and the fact that he neither really wanted, nor would ever be able to broach that abyss.

XIII

That morning on the beach he had found, miraculously, a thatched umbrella with nobody under it. Due to the unexpected shade, he felt an immediate obligation to read, but remembered that he had brought no book. So he lay down on his stomach, his face on his folded arms, and looked around just once for Tessa. But she was nowhere. He shut his eyes.

He tried very hard not to think of her, so he thought about what he would say to Terence about her. Then he thought about Terence. Then he thought very briefly about his schools, past and present.

He had been sent off to boarding school, as all his friends had been, at the very first opportunity. The school had a grand reputation which his parents could ill afford. He was quite happy there and rarely saw his parents. Once he came home and said: "My friend Terence has been looking up his family tree."

His parents looked aghast, his father at his mother, and the other way around, so he had not dared continue.

But another time he came home and asked: "Mummy, do we have any blue blood in the family?"

(Obviously, he couldn't help himself.) In any case, that was the end of *that* school. Now he went to a dour one in Wales, which he enjoyed very much indeed and which, he was told, taught him all the proper values (whatever they were, he didn't quite know; but he tried to cherish them wherever he happened to be — even when he was with the Duperrex).

"Mais, Larry, où se trouve Wales?" (Madame Duperrex, in a commendably honest moment.)

He even tried to uphold those famous values when he

sighed for Tessa; but they were all wrong for her. Tessa the Beloved, with all the soot around her cat's eyes and a white flower in her dripping hair. Tessa, who, under an almost untenable burden of beauty, ate, laughed, dipped, sunned, lived, and loved (whom and what did she love?) on a lazy, separate, passive, and yet desperate level of intensity.

Tessa in bed. Larry, numbed at first by her lightness, his lightness, their combined weightlessness. Her face thrown back, spilled in the silence of the room, striped by alternate light and shade admitted through the shutters. Her face — flat nose, square chin, strong mouth — offered. Proffered even. Her eyes shut. Long, ovoid eyelids, a double crescent of soot and lashes. Hair spread out in the shape of a fan. Both pillows on the floor. Naked: he held her naked, without her bikini. White breasts, hardly etched except for their dark cores as she lay flat against the rumpled whiteness of the sheet. Did she moan? In Italian? Was she silent? Totally silent? Did she sigh and turn her head away from him, just once?

Lone Larry, under the thatched umbrella, braced himself violently, gathered his long legs under him, ran toward the water as fast as he could, stumbled on a large but inoffensive obstacle, and fell headlong, at last, into the sea.

He was a strong swimmer and knew that he was admired by the crowd that went in for dips and seemed to have nothing better to do than stand and watch him from the beach. He swam halfway to a small island that looked like a comma, thought that Tessa had perhaps arrived, turned around, and swam back to shore.

Under the thatched umbrella, his heart beat heavily against one of Madame Duperrex' none too clean, rented towels. At last he recovered his breath and turned onto his right elbow in order to check the Italian situation.

He was startled by an unknown face, burned very red by the sun. A pair of slightly bloodshot gray eyes, set wide apart, watched him closely from under an old straw hat with a frayed brim that was not unlike the thatched umbrella that now sheltered them both.

A polite voice inquired in English: "Are you expecting anyone?"

"No, no," said Larry, suddenly shy as only an English adolescent can be shy.

"May I install myself?" asked the voice.

"Of course," said Larry.

The woman did just that. She was tall, big boned, and of a certain age. She unrolled a mud brown towel, sat down, surrounded herself with all sorts of possessions, took off a sweater, and, still wearing a longish broomstick skirt, stretched herself out on her stomach with her arms at her side.

"How lovely," she said, and immediately went to sleep.

After a while, Larry got up and went to the very edge of the water to look around for Sam, the world's most accomplished destroyer of sand castles. As he was nowhere to be seen, Larry began to build an endlessly convoluted and drippy structure that started off with canals and thick towers that would eventually grow thinner and thinner, until he would reduce them to a single drop of wet sand. He had it all figured out in his head, but he did not get very far.

Tessa, her feet in the water, stood not far from him. Even from the back, she looked sullen. She wore an inky blue bikini so brief that the demarcation line of her buttocks was clearly visible, and Larry saw that she was evenly tanned all over. Did they strip in the Italian Enclosure? No. The mood of that particular beach went in the direction of minimal clothing and maximal decorum. Larry stared at

Tessa's mole, until the water being obviously too frigid for her that day, she turned around, made a face at Larry, and walked on. It was obvious to him that she would have made a face no matter who it was that crouched on the wet sand and looked up at her, be it a dog or a distinguished-looking gentleman with prematurely gray hair, although what he would be doing crouching, Larry did not know. Well, picking up seashells maybe, although they were few and far between. There were so few, all over the world; all over the beaches, everywhere in the world, there were fewer and fewer seashells.

Tessa had on Francesco's suede string with the charm against the evil eye wrapped around her left wrist, and the fingers of her right hand were a mass of gold rings — animal's heads, abstract ones, Larry could make out one convoluted snake.

Tessa lay face down on a towel next to her friend Marisa. Larry walked back to his thatched umbrella. The woman in the broomstick skirt appeared to be fast asleep. He saw Marco, who wandered about like a lost soul, his Moroccan hand patting him on the back as he walked.

Larry lay down, his chin on both his fists. He had a direct, perfect, although foreshortened view of Tessa.

After a while, Marisa sat up, took a round, pharmaceutical-looking mirror from inside a Sabena flight bag, balanced it and its stem on her knees, took her long mass of hair in her hands, drew it back, pulled it up, twisted it, twisted it again, and slowly pinned it against her neat head with large hair-pins that she hand-picked from her mouth. Then she engulfed the result into a dark pink bathing cap, abloom with many-petaled rubber flowers. This took a very long time.

The woman in the broomstick skirt suddenly sat up and said: "What a nice sleep." And put the ragged straw hat back on her head.

"I must get some sun on my back," she suddenly decided, and moved out of the umbrella's shadow to sit crosslegged, her back to the sea, her front to the restaurant.

There she sat on her mud brown towel, silent for a while.

Then she addressed Larry, while he wondered, Do I look so English that she never even hesitated?

"Do you know? I was here two years ago, and there were three of us on this beach, naked. Now there must be three hundred. I find it very depressing."

Larry watched Tessa and Marisa. Francesco stood over them half blocking the view, his weight on one leg, the palms of his hands flat against his thighs.

"See that Italian couple in the restaurant?" the woman asked.

Larry looked; it was Tessa's mother and father.

"They've been coming to the island for years," she said. Then: "They look thoroughly worn-out, undone. Spent. Surely they must be younger than they look. Something went desperately wrong somewhere; and it wasn't a family tragedy — a child with a congenital defect further mangled by a Fiat, you know what I mean. No, it happened during the war, probably. They must have been rabid fascists, or antifascists. It really comes to the same in the end, certainly as far as their looks go."

And suddenly, she turned her head toward Larry, hat and all.

"D'you follow?"

Larry nodded out of politeness, up and down.

"What does fascism mean to you, I wonder?"

Now he felt trapped. As if he were Terence with his psychologist. Except that this was something outside him, that he should know about. The woman appeared to be a professional investigator, doctor, teacher, or lawyer.

"Oh, I don't know," said Larry.

The woman was silent; right elbow on her towel, right hand on her hat, she waited.

"Brown Shirts? Mussolini?" she offered, after a time.

Larry did not answer. There was talk of fascism in school, but Larry was not really interested; perhaps because he thought it beyond him. Students his age did not participate. Besides, it had not been about Brown Shirts and Mussolini. That came under Modern History.

Larry had overheard his masters and much older students, and what they talked about was American Imperialism and how it wrecked whatever it touched. Greece, for example. It was the Americans, one older student had affirmed, and no one else who needed the colonels. Was that true? Possibly, although it certainly *sounded* biased. In any case, what difference did it make?

For the effect of that statement over the general landscape and well-being of the Cycladic isles that particular summer was one that Larry did not even wish to begin to contemplate. "D'Annunzio?" Larry suddenly said, out of where he did not know. (His mother addressing a reputable London novelist in her sitting room: ". . . and that tiny poet with his delusions of grandeur was in a way the most appalling fascist of them all.")

(Whatever that was. Larry had no idea; he had simply retained the name.)

"I see," said the woman, and lay her head on the towel once more, while Tessa's mother and father peacefully sat in the restaurant and ate in perfect communion from a large dish of fruit salad. Large, delicately tinted chunks of green melon, called peppino, cantaloupe, and watermelon, each pierced with a toothpick. (Agincourt!) They did look lined and worn, although Larry did not see what fascism could possibly have had to do with it.

XIV

Larry looked toward foreshortened Tessa. Marisa of the flowered cap nudged Francesco with her foot, shouted encouragement, offered him both her hands, and he drew her up. Hand in hand, they ran toward the sea. Marisa, with water up to her calves, stopped. From that moment on, she proceeded very carefully. She whimpered, and hesitated, and uttered little cries, and held her breasts for comfort until she made it — up to her neck. Francesco ran and dived, head tucked between his arms, but after this impressive beginning, he surfaced immediately and settled into a stately breast-stroke, as if he were an elderly professor from another age attacking the Lake of Lugano in pince-nez and goatee. Sandro still lay on the beach on his stomach, still glistening like a seal from his last swim.

Larry decided it was time to go back into the water. But the woman, as on a signal, turned to him and said:

"You know, I have only just arrived. Yesterday, to be exact. And now I have to be off again — Zurich. Now, you lie here and it's a fact of life that Zurich simply does not exist. But I must nevertheless start to make my way there tomorrow. It's for my daughter, you see. My father-in-law wants her to go to a finishing school. He finds her rough. She's with and on horses all day long and half the night, and I give her complete freedom. What *total* nonsense. A *finishing* school. What is your opinion of a finishing school for girls, in our day and age?"

Larry thought, but was not given time to answer.

"I don't see why you should have to express an opinion," the woman said. "I shall simply make certain I don't find the right one, if such a thing is to be found. But at the same

time I must bring back proof that I tried. My father-in-law
is a tyrant at death's door and they are the most dismal sort
of tyrant you can find."

With this, she appeared satisfied. She turned on her bottom until she faced the sea and quite emphatically thrust
her chin out to the sun.

Larry decided not to go for a swim, partly because Tessa
had never been so near.

Now she applied more soot around her eyes and lipgloss to
her lips. She went for a short dip, submerged, emerged,
and walked out again. She brushed out her wet hair with
a tiny black lacquer brush.

The sun had begun to slip; so did the afternoon.

The woman stood up and cheerfully told Larry: "Well,
it's time for a swim." She paused. "Then I'll go into town to
buy a charm against the evil eye and a hand-woven bed-
spread for the inevitable newlyweds back home. They ship,
you know. Takes about six months from here to Capetown."

She dropped her broomstick skirt, carefully stepped out
of it, and left it, in the shape of an abandoned parachute.

Larry looked up to see that the strap of the woman's
bathing suit had slipped far down her arm. He looked down
again.

"Whoops," she said, and wriggled her shoulder as she replaced it. Then she ran into the sea.

The sun had lost its power to warm. Larry came out in
goose pimples and reached for his shirt. A chill swept over
the entire beach. Two small caïques, brightly striped like
toys, waited in the shallow water. Two sailors shrilly adver-
tised their destination. It was identical: another beach, from
which a bus came and went.

In unison, an older couple walked into the restaurant's two
toilets in order to change.

A young homosexual trio pulled three jellabas over their heads and saw to it that they fell correctly, first on themselves and then on one another.

Tessa started to chatter and poked at Sandro's naked back.

The woman, panting energetically, ran toward the thatched umbrella she had shared with Larry. She wrapped herself in her sandy towel, collected all her belongings, amiably wished Larry good-bye, and a moment later, nimbly hoisted herself (with the help of a sailor's brown hand) onto one of the two caïques.

Francesco had gone to sleep in a sanded alley by the Italian Enclosure. Tall rushes of bamboo threw agitated shadows over him, but he slept on, exhausted. Larry suspected that he hardly went to bed at night. Every day, he came to the beach, drained at noon. He left it rested at five. He had been asleep for a long time.

Now Tessa moved toward sleeping Francesco. Larry watched her lazy walk and waited for her to wake him. But she did not. She hesitated. She walked halfway around him, and still he did not wake. She waited for a second, on the verge of action. Then, resolutely, she sat down on her haunches and, with the long, unpainted nail of her right index finger, slowly scratched out a message for him in the sand.

And Larry thought that no love letter he would ever come across in his future life, no actual treason could possibly equal that unexpected moment of cold jealousy. The sight of Tessa, primitively crouched by her brother's sleeping face, tenderly spelling her secret message for him in the sand.

At that moment, Larry decided to leave. But Francesco lazily rolled over on his back and sleepily, almost instinctively, put his hand out, touched his sister's head, and fingered a long strand of her hair, until she laughed at him, because he had just belched with his eyes still shut. Then she stood up and extended her hands, palms inward, toward his. Francesco grabbed her wrists instead; she stumbled, but by then he had jumped up with a moan. Tessa chose to forget her message and clasp him in her arms instead.

Marisa had wrapped a length of Indian cotton around her waist and pulled a man's sweater over her head. Busily, she packed her Sabena flight bag. Sandro fitted in his camera.

The two caïques had gone off, and so Larry, rather than wait for their return trip, decided to go up the donkey path instead. So, apparently, did the Italians, because, as Francesco stood by silently and rubbed his eyes, picked up his sandals, and yawned, the rest of the group, with many superfluous gestures and a great deal of talk, decided that it was very late, that *they* were very late, that they could walk up and try to catch the bus at the road crossing. (A facultative stop.)

Larry walked just ahead of them. On a long crescent of beach, the incessant chatter behind him revolved around Marco. And it was true that Marco had disappeared and that his disappearance seemed to be cause for concern, either because he was so unpredictable, or because they were Italians and liked to make a fuss.

The donkey path wound sharply up the cliff. It was steep terrain, truly difficult to manage: dusty, slippery, riddled with sharp stones that rolled underfoot and donkey excrement that also rolled and felt even more distressing to Larry, who had decided he would get a better grip without the slippery leather soles of his sandals. The wind blew dust into his mouth and eyes. He paused; he was quite out of breath.

Behind him, Tessa complained and sighed and moaned, while Sandro tried to comfort her. "Aaaah!" she sighed, and then "Oh!" she cried, and the "Oh!" appeared to be some sort of an emergency, for Larry could feel them stop behind him. But he did not want to turn around.

Shortly afterward, the climb was resumed. Larry adjusted his pace. If only Tessa were in front, so that he could see her, or next to him, so that he could help her: clasp her waist, as in a dance, and effortlessly — or so it always appears — lift her to the top of the hill.

Larry was first to stand by the paved road and spot a bus slowly wind its way toward them from quite, quite far. By the time it reached them, Larry was surrounded by Italians. They dropped everything they held and raised their arms high and shouted and screamed, but the bus, so dense with people that there was not a crack of light to be seen, simply rode by while the driver lifted his hands off the steering wheel in a gesture of total surrender; as if it were not within his mortal powers to stop the vehicle at all.

The Italians collapsed. It was as if they had miraculously survived some natural calamity, only to find that human help was not forthcoming.

Tessa, all adroop, sat down on a rounded stone at the edge of the donkey path. Sandro immediately found his camera in Marisa's bag and kneeled to take pictures of Tessa.

Larry looked at the Italians, each of them in turn. None of them looked back at him. In spite of his fight against wind and dust and the fact that he was uncomfortable from head to foot, they managed to make him feel completely transparent.

They all spoke at the same time, in Italian, of course. To walk down the paved road, all the way to the other beach, where the bus *had* to stop in order to turn around, was much too far, Francesco said. Tessa would never make it. To stumble back down the donkey path in order to take a caïque that would bring them to that same other beach was beyond reason, said Marisa. Tessa muttered something about the bus, which Larry did not understand, and then they all seemed to cheer up. Sandro now photographed the double rainbow of the caïques on their return trip over the undulant sea below. He obviously had color film in his camera. Francesco said that Marco had probably returned earlier, with his parents. Tessa approved. This idea was greeted with relief by everyone. Francesco adjusted his belt, and Tessa her rings. She seemed to have added several to that morning's loot. One was a gold ram's head.

The wind blew. Tessa found a pink shirt in her beach bag and put it on. Slowly, she rolled up the sleeves and tied the shirttails around her waist; then she looked down into her bosom and started to button the shirt up, very slowly. Francesco watched her carefully. So did Sandro. So did Marisa, who seemed to be very very young, much younger than Tessa — fifteen perhaps.

Sandro took more photographs of Tessa. She licked her lips and posed, profile, hair afloat behind her. It was then that Larry realized how well she knew how terribly lovely she was, and how much everyone else, never mind him, was conscious of the same fact.

They were interrupted by the bus. It suddenly charged full speed up the dusty road in the opposite direction from which it had come and stopped directly at the opening to the donkey path.

"Aaaah!" everyone said, including Larry. It was a miracle. The driver crossed his arms on his chest, opened his doors, and beamed, while his load alternatively laughed, protested, or raged in several languages.

Marisa raised herself into the open front door. So did Larry, although his progress was arrested at the bottom step, where he stood flattened out against Marisa. But she managed to rise again, and so did he, and the door closed. Francesco's voice was heard once, half laugh, half scream. Larry extricated his right hand from Marisa's right breast and managed to extend it around her shoulders.

The heat was untenable, the road dusty, the deeply winding turns unexpected. Also, the ride was extremely bumpy, particularly for those who had to stand. Marisa turned slightly so that she was pinned flat against Larry. Neither one of them had anything to hold on to, but there seemed to be so many people on that middle step that it did not matter. Larry held Marisa, and she squinted as she smiled up at him.

After one extremely precarious turn, a group of young Frenchmen began to shout obscenities at the driver, in French naturally. The *bouzouki* blared. The driver, who wore a moribund flower behind his ear and seemed to be in excellent spirits, turned off his radio in order not to miss the fun and took over the song himself. He drove and sang and kept his eyes on the bumpy road, while directly above his head, a string of talismans, charms against the evil eye, icons, and individual snapshots of his children, his wife, and probable nephews and nieces either slid back and forth — depending on the terrain — or danced up and down.

The French soon began to quarrel among themselves. There was a scuffle; a woman screamed. The driver laughed, for he knew there was no space for anything much to develop.

Marisa had thick lashes and for some reason kept her eyes closed for most of the trip. She wore a crystal heart on a thin gold chain tight around her neck. At one point, she opened her eyes, squinted at Larry, and smiled again. It was an angelic smile. But the next moment, the bus lurched around a corner and they were thrown together. Nothing happened. Marisa managed to slip a thin arm around his neck. They looked to the rest of the world (the busload) like lovers.

She managed to move her head back in order to say to him, by way of explanation, with an Italian lilt to her French (so . . . she thought he was French): "On va sûrement tomber quand il ouvrira les portes."

But they did not. They jumped down sideways, neatly, with their arms still about each other. But then they had to run because of the crowd that flowed out implacably behind them.

xv

In the village square by the docks, Tessa, Francesco, and Sandro stood together and chattered and laughed. Francesco, still barefoot, laughed so hard he was doubled in two. Obviously, there had been happenings at the back of the bus that had necessarily escaped the front. Marisa hobbled on one leg for a while (did she have a cramp?) but soon joined the others. (Was Sandro a brother? A cousin? A friend? A half brother, perhaps.) She did not say goodbye or give Larry so much as a backward glance.

Francesco and Tessa, with their arms wrapped around each other's waists, walked off rapidly and soon turned into a side street. Marisa and Sandro walked behind, appeared to hesitate, then resolutely moved into the crowd that walked the docks.

Larry did not go home for fear of immediate reemployment. But he could not remember when he had felt more lonely. He did not know what to do with himself. For a while, he had been part of a larger design (the Italian circle), and now he knew, more than ever before, that it was impossible for an outsider to join in — unless one Italian momentarily dropped the other's hand while dancing in the round.

Barefoot, wind-blown, cold, his towel wrapped around the three hundred drachmas he had so far managed to keep but was terrified to lose, Larry wandered from shop to shop around the docks. In and out he walked, as all the doors were kept open.

In one of the travel agencies, an elegant young Frenchman ordered a helicopter to take him to the mainland, but the young woman behind the desk told him that he was overweight; that is, that he had too much luggage. The young man began to stamp his feet. The young woman was firm. The young man said she would be sorry. He proceeded to make a scene, spat as he shouted that he had many friends in the government and had been personally received by Papadopoulos. (Lots of spitting here.) The young woman only watched him calmly from behind thick glasses, so the young man shifted tactics. In a perfectly normal tone of voice, he requested immediate use of the telephone. Larry fled.

He passed a fat orthodox priest with a square beard, who ate an ice-cream cone that dribbled. He crossed the three men in jellabas, who walked at the edge of the pier, all three beautifully wind-blown.

For the wind had risen again. In the port, a small fleet of caïques was stranded. Light as corks, contrapuntally, they bobbed up and down.

Larry watched them. So lovely, each one painted differently in alternating stripes of primary colors.

After much reflection, Larry bought a very large and complicated sponge that looked like a sculpture for his mother (an extravagance) and a key ring with a charm against the evil eye for his father (a bargain, but the charm might amuse him, and besides, his father always complained of either lost or mislaid key rings and keys).

Then Larry remembered Terence, and immediately decided to forget him. He would bring him a matchbox with a phoenix and a soldier on it.

The woman on the beach had made him reflect. Now he wondered whether he shouldn't read up on Italy, Greece, *and* fascism. He knew just enough to know that he knew nothing. Perhaps his father's encyclopedia would suffice. But he did wonder: Beyond the kind women who knitted, the Italian circle, the sailors with enormous hands and feet, the four Duperrex in their rented house, the touching tailor in steel-rimmed glasses who sewed in semidarkness the livelong day — on the mainland in general and in Athens in particular — what exactly went on? Should he interrogate Monsieur Duperrex? Surely this could wait until evening.

Larry decided to sit outside at a taverna by the docks. The wind immediately blew his package off the round table. (It contained both the sponge and the key ring.) He ran after it, but a man in a sailor's cap had already caught it. He handed it back to Larry with a conspiratorial smile.

Now, with the package firmly anchored by his bare feet under the table, Larry ordered a Greek coffee. Only it was Turkish coffee, a souvenir of the long occupation. He loved the doll-sized cups. Half the mixture in it was dregs; he liked a half a teaspoon of that. It tasted like gritty coffee mud, and half a teaspoon was all he could manage, so he switched to the tall glass of ice water that was automatically served with the coffee. He was about to go inside to get a plate of cucumber-and-yogurt salad when he saw the woman he had met and left at the beach.

"Hullo," he shouted (because of the wind) as she walked by. (And suddenly flushed.)

"What *are* you doing?" she asked.

"Nothing," he said.

"Well, come along. I'm off to Delos. Have you been?"

"No," said Larry.

"Well, hurry along."

Larry was under the table gathering package, towel, and sandals.

"Take everything with you; come along now," the woman said.

Larry paid and fell in step with her. She still had her broomstick skirt on — also the frayed straw hat, a sweater, of the kind the Ariadnes of the island knitted, a pair of sneakers, and a free-form straw bag decorated by a half moon in plastic painted to look like a slice of watermelon.

"Karalombo is an old friend," she said. "He's taking over a party of Italians." (Here Larry's heart did something strange: it plunged and then rolled over like a wave about to hit the shore.) "No more than half a dozen," she said, "and he's got a huge caïque. I'm quite certain his party won't mind."

She looked over. Larry fought both the wind and his own thoughts.

"Come on," the woman said, "we're late as it is. Don't drag your feet." (It was hard to tell whether or not she was serious.)

Now the wind rose as they passed by the two armed soldiers who stood on each side of the entrance to the wharf. It looked exactly like a stage set: a flimsy gateway made of wood and painted a watery aqua with a cut-out phoenix on top. The woman smiled at one of the men and explained to him, in Greek, all about herself and Larry and Karalombo. The man smiled; there was no problem. They walked onto the pier; for a moment Larry thought (and in a way hoped) that he would be blown off the pier. They soon reached the caïque. It was the largest one Larry had ever seen, and Karalombo greeted them with such genuine joy that Larry knew that he was indeed an old friend and that he would not charge the woman anything. Larry was introduced, Karalombo shook hands. His hand was callused and dry. He helped the woman onto the caïque. Larry managed by himself.

It was then that Tessa smiled at him.

"It's that Italian group that was on the beach earlier on," the woman explained to Larry.

Tessa sat between her mother and Sandro. Marisa whispered into Francesco's ear and giggled. Marco, in his eternal black bathing trunks and a wine dark windbreaker, stood up and walked toward the sailor's closed cabin. Tessa put her right arm through her mother's, looked at Larry carefully, blinked slowly once, and lay her moody head on her mother's shoulder. Her father was not on the boat.

In the same continuous rush of emotion, Larry wanted to run toward Tessa and run back to the docks. By the time he had put himself together again, they were out at sea and Theodora had decided to introduce herself.

XVI

As the caïque approached Delos, Larry thought they were about to reach their destination. But he was wrong. The island, bare and forbidding and totally deserted, offered no shelter, no possible mooring place, and the caïque simply moved past it.

Now it hugged the coast to its left, peacefully, and Larry fell into that pleasant passive state that comes from following a coastline after having been at sea, and watching land pass slowly by. He was soon interrupted.

"Those are new; they weren't up two years ago," Theodora half shouted. She sounded disturbed.

Larry saw three stucco houses, perched at random on a cliff near the shore. One had a palm tree by its side; another, a line with a lot of white washing on it.

"That's strange," said Theodora. "Nobody's supposed to live on that island. Oh, well — guides or guards . . ." she hesitated.

A moment later: "The museum," she announced, and pointed to it, which was unnecessary. It was a large, long building tinted pinky yellow, the decreed uniform for official structures in hot climates. It was also totally nondescript, except that it looked as if it had been finished yesterday and not yet opened to the public. It was, in fact, closed.

"Always reminds me of Castro's Cuba," said Theodora above the sound of the motor. "Except that I've never been there."

Larry saw the museum go by and dismissed it. It was at that moment that he became conscious of the ruins; except that they did not look like ruins at first. What he saw was devastation: an enormous field of dark gray rubble. Then the caïque veered sharply to the left and his stomach heaved so violently that he automatically came out of his pleasantly contemplative state.

He looked at his watch. The crossing had taken an hour and thirteen minutes, instead of the predicted fifty-two in heavy seas.

Tessa, huddled against her mother, slowly blinking, eyes half-closed, long hair afloat in the wind, had remained silent. Francesco had alternately slept and brooded. Marco had managed to walk back and forth between his seat at the back of the caïque and the sailor's cabin. Marisa and Sandro had taken turns shouting in each other's ear, as they both had soft voices.

Now all around them the water was calm. Utterly calm. They were in port. They had arrived.

Marco, rope in hand, was the first one to jump off the caïque. He helped Karalombo tie up. The boat was much too large for one man to manage alone. The sailor's forehead was beaded with sweat that fell onto his eyelashes and then ran down his cheeks like tears.

"Of course you know the port is sacred," Theodora said as soon as she had stepped onto the pier.

"I don't know *anything* about Delos," Larry answered firmly for once. He wanted his position made absolutely clear.

He and Theodora were the last to disembark.

Tessa's mother stood unmoving on the pier. She nodded politely at Theodora, who reciprocated. Larry thought that she might be waiting for Karalombo to finish with the rope so that she might ask him something.

The two women looked at each other and behaved as if they had not been destined to meet in the first place, but Fate, or Whoever, having made a mistake by throwing them together — onto the same caïque in this instance — had also forced them, after a while, to acknowledge each other's presence without having been introduced.

On one side of the pier, neatly stacked one on top of the other, were two large, wooden crates neatly and completely filled with empty Coca-Cola bottles.

At the end of that same pier, on a patch of dried-out grass, two soldiers dressed in khaki and fully armed stood stiffly at attention by a wooden booth that looked like the inside of a matchbox standing up.

As soon as the caïque was safely tied up and he had exchanged a few words with Tessa's mother, Karalombo ran up to the two soldiers. A moment later, they were at ease. In fact, as soon as the sailor started to talk to them, they became convulsed with laughter.

Nearby, a large wooden billboard proclaimed in four languages (Greek, French, English, and German) that it was strictly forbidden to take anything away (". . . even the smallest thing . . .") from the archeological site. Larry shuddered and looked down; a lizard, fat and dry, had just run over his almost bare left foot and disappeared into a clump of grass. He looked up again.

Theodora adjusted her hat. Francesco tugged at Tessa's hair and said something that made her laugh. Only there was no mirth in Tessa's laughter; never did her face look as cruel as when she laughed. She reached for Francesco's hair and, in turn, pulled it.

Acquiescently, their mother looked on. She appeared to be familiar with the island of Delos, with the ways of her children, and also with those of Marco, Sandro, and Marisa, whatever they were to her.

Marco walked up to Tessa and put his arm resolutely around her bare shoulders, as if he had appointed himself her official guide. Only she didn't look as if she needed a guide. She had looked particularly blank ever since she had set foot on Delos — blank and bored. Moreover, she looked as if nothing, from now on, could possibly distract her.

Theodora looked at her and sighed. "How beautiful the young are today," she said. Larry hoped that her own daughter was not particularly ugly, or deformed or something. Well, it couldn't be anything very serious if she spent all her days and half her nights on a horse.

It was obvious that Theodora was a great walker.

Tessa acknowledged Larry's presence on a new island with a nod, as he and Theodora went ahead. The look that accompanied the nod was not devoid of sarcasm. Oh God, Larry thought, although he wasn't really thinking of God at all. What must she think? First the elder Duperrex; then Jean-Marc and Daniel-Georges; then Sam, storming and stampeding the sand castle he had helped them build; then the scene that inevitably followed. And now Mrs. Theodora White from Capetown, a teacher of biology well into her fifties.

Larry looked away and all around him. He saw a vast, flat wasteland, and the tall hill beyond. He saw fields of wild wheat bowed into tall arcs by the wind. He still saw rubble, but closer up, it was no longer the same deep gray. It had grown paler, more golden, dappled with pink and sun.

He looked down and saw an amphora, lying all pitted, prone on the saffron grass. What was it doing there? A curved body, a shattered arm. It looked like an odalisque. As he walked on, the wide fields of stone began to take shape and move toward him. (Of course, he was the one who moved toward *them*.) Soon he walked on cobbled streets instead of bare ground, and they were neatly defined between rows of beautifully proportioned houses that had been reduced to floor plans that faced the sky. Pieces of column stood neatly stacked in the corner of a room. And in the distance, like exclamation marks, stood the tall columns: with their capitals on; without their capitals; in formation or alone.

They had entered the Sacred City.

Larry found himself in front of several oil vats of such impressive size that any one of them could have hidden the most rotund of Ali Baba's thieves; and they all seemed to be intact. Only it felt more like a cemetery than a city — a cemetery of stones under which not a single human being was buried.

"Such a lovely day!" said Theodora. "This *should* be an experience. You may, and then again you may not, get anything out of it. But I don't think you will ever forget."

The Italians, vastly overtaken, lingered behind. Tessa and her mother sat on broken columns as if they were two kitchen stools. Marco had strayed and stood stooped over an imperceptible something on the grass.

Larry looked to his left; they had passed the museum. He let himself be guided inland.

Theodora: "Do you know that in England, in the eighteenth century, the fashionable thing to have was a Greek temple at the bottom of your garden? So the temples were built and then broken up on the spot for the sake of reality. After that, a monk was imported. Anyone would do, you understand, so long as he was Greek and made the sign of the cross from right to left instead of from left to right — across the chest, I mean. His costume was, of course, provided. Anyway, the monk walked around his temple against the setting sun, and genuflected, and everyone was wildly happy. The real ruins came later," she added wistfully. Larry had no idea what she meant. Theodora turned around.

"I think they're going toward the theater." She looked down at her watch and up at Larry. "No matter. This way you'll see the temples to the foreign deities, or perhaps we won't; we have to make it all very short. But this is my favorite part of the island."

She stopped, inhaled deeply, chin up, and said: "Thank God for the meltémi. It rarely blows on the island. Two years ago when I came, it was so hot and still that I had to go for a swim. Just *couldn't* go on. And by the time we were through with the guided tour, two kind men practically had to *carry* me back to the boat."

Larry couldn't imagine Theodora being carried off by anyone at any time, except if she had just broken a leg or her back, but he was just old enough and diplomatic enough to let her have her feminine moment.

"The so-called Captain's House, to your left. It has a mosaic with an anchor on it."

She walked right on, past it. But then she suddenly stopped, put her bag down, and brought out her *Guide Bleu*. Larry wished she hadn't. She must have left the ribbon marker in the right place, because the book fell open to Delos, and Theodora carefully unfolded the map and began, once more, to study it. A moment passed before she said: "You realize we did this all wrong."

Larry laughed. He knew she wouldn't mind and he felt all joyous again. On that particular afternoon, his moods seemed to vacillate according to the ways of the wind, the light, the sea, the camouflaged lizards, and the up-and-down movements of Tessa's bare heels in the sandals she had worn in the village square so long ago it seemed, an eternity away, and yet just earlier on, that same afternoon.

"It doesn't matter at all. It just happens *not* to be the way I did it last time."

She folded her map again, shut the *Guide Bleu*, picked up her bag with her left hand, but kept the book in her right, like a missal, with its ribbon marker showing.

"It's obviously very easy to get lost here," she said. (A safe enough remark.) She turned to Larry, and with an unexpected note of despair in her voice: "There's so much to *see*. I always promise myself that I shall stay overnight. I want to see the sunrise. They have three or four beds in what they call the Tourist Pavilion over there by the museum — I just never have the time."

They walked on.

"Ah! The House of Dionysus, famed — "

"But I hear voices!" Larry interrupted.

"You're right! Absolutely right!"

It was an elegant, if somewhat crowded house.

For the Italians, on that seemingly totally deserted island, had somehow managed to materialize (out of a well? a cistern? an oil-vat?) a four-foot guide dressed in khaki with a cap on the back of his head, who now stopped his tirade about a mosaic spread at their feet like a rug under the Aegean sky to request a cigarette from Tessa's mother. He carried a great number of keys on a steel ring, and Larry now understood the advantage of organized guided tours, and the fact that Theodora had accepted to visit Delos (and so had the Italians, but did it matter much to them?) knowing she would not be able to enter certain houses. Tessa's mother lit the guide's cigarette with a gold lighter, and he bowed his gratitude before resuming his speech.

Marco walked in and out of the columns of the peristyle as if he were a ponderous child doing a daisy chain. In a corner, on the edge of a well, sat Francesco. As for Marisa and Tessa, they had climbed a flight of marble steps and now stood chattering on a small platform that was all that was left of what must have been the second story of the house.

"Dionysus' ladder," said Theodora.

Marisa gaily waved down at Sandro, who knelt below, one eye shut, taking photographs of them with his Minox.

"This is quite incredible," said Theodora, slightly peeved, as she surveyed the scene.

"How did they get here?" Larry asked wonderingly. "I thought they were behind us."

"They must have gone around; and we chatted a lot."

We? Larry thought, but of course kept silent. He was so

happy, so terribly happy; now they would all continue the tour together.

The guide spoke in some sort of bastard Italian, but no one seemed to pay attention except Theodora, who said: "Rubbish! For goodness' sake don't listen to him; guides never know anything."

After a while, Tessa and Marisa descended and Francesco got up. Marco was recalled from his daisy chain, the guide showed everyone out, and carefully locked the rusty steel door.

"La casa di Cleopatra!" The guide waved them in. At this point, Larry, who had been trying to follow, became totally lost.

"An Athenian Cleopatra." Theodora came to the rescue. "And our little party has been reinforced!"

Two heavily draped but headless statues, framed by low walls on both sides and carefully roped off, stood against the sky. And in front of them, a trousered woman was being photographed. She appeared embarrassed by the sudden arrival of the group. She toned down her pose, and ran her right hand through her short gray hair, while another woman, with an identical haircut but in a skirt and espadrilles and a camera slung about her neck, took a step back. She was not satisfied.

"Un peu plus à gauche," she said firmly, with an explanatory to-the-left gesture of the left hand. She continued to look down her chest, into the viewer. She was concentrating extremely hard and did not appear to notice that she was no longer alone with her companion, while the woman who posed had become self-conscious and once more ran her hand through her hair.

The shutter clicked, and without looking up the woman in espadrilles began to wind the handle with exaggerated dexterity and said, "Bravo! Parfait!"

Marisa and Tessa started to giggle. The woman with the camera removed it from her neck, advanced toward her trousered companion, and they exchanged roles, so that now the second woman posed, shorter and stouter than the first.

The guide rumbled on, the cigarette in the corner of his mouth getting shorter and shorter. Larry wondered whether he would soon ask for another one. Careful not to disturb the two Frenchwomen, he walked over to have a good look at the decapitated statues.

They stood on a wide pedestal inscribed at length in Cyrillic. They were lovely, standing there in the wind. One was male and the other female. The male statue had an additional plinth under it that brought the base of its neck up to the height of its mate's, like wearing elevated shoes. But as Larry looked again, he saw that the man had no feet at all. His toga was shorter than his companion's, and so his bare ankles, exposed to the "assault of centuries," must at some point have given way, whereas the woman's draperies fell heavily to the ground, thus reinforcing her stand.

The woman in espadrilles struck a new and bolder pose. Marisa poked Tessa's shoulder blade; Tessa looked back and started to giggle.

Tessa's mother said something inaudible but imperative above the voice of the guide, and both girls shut up.

"Generation gap," said Theodora. "Actually, I find those two women ludicrous, don't you?"

Instead of answering, suddenly, unexpectedly, Larry also burst out laughing. And very loud. Everything stopped. Everybody looked. The guide closed his mouth over the butt of his cigarette and so fell silent too.

Marisa giggled again. Larry, head bowed, walked out of Cleopatra's house with as few steps as he could manage. It was the only way he thought he could calm down.

In a moment he was back. Theodora was waiting for him. "In case you haven't got it all down, the headless woman is Cleopatra and the man is her husband, Dioscourides. Don't listen to anything the guide says. Do you understand Italian?"

"Hardly," said Larry, watching an upside-down lizard descending the face of a wall at full speed.

"So much the better," Theodora said. "The date on the pedestal is one hundred thirty-seven B.C. A touching monument to marital constancy."

The note in her voice was so frankly sardonic that Larry decided she must be very unhappily married if her husband was still alive or if they had not been divorced. That would explain her travels, the bitterness over the father-in-law, and the fact that she had not spoken of a husband in the first place. But then, why should she have, in the space of half a day?

The point was that on that particular afternoon Larry had found the time to feel that he had just begun to understand certain things.

The four-foot guide said something about Cleopatra and her husband having been very rich, and Tessa's mother opened her purse and gave him a coin. He took off his cap and thanked her effusively.

"*Andiamo!*" he said like a good Greek guide, and carried them off, leaving behind the two Frenchwomen and their camera.

Headed by the guide, the little group walked inland. But after about thirty steps, Theodora stopped.

"The lions," she said. And opened her left arm wide and pointed beyond the museum with the index finger of her left hand.

"Can you see them? You look twenty-twenty. Over there.

They face the Sacred Lake on that terrace. Can't you see them?"

The traffic behind them had come to a halt.

"Let them pass," Theodora ordered. Francesco and Sandro silently moved up.

"Never mind. You can have an even better view of them further up." (How kind she was.)

For Larry had always experienced a moment of panic whenever he had been required to "see" something. The something had always turned out to be so fleeting . . .

("Larry! Look! A flopsy bunny! . . .") His mother, of course. And there had been no flopsy bunny. No bunny anywhere. They had stood in a field, Larry no taller than the tall grass. And the flopsy bunny must have been a very fast hare.

("Larry! Look! A shooting-star! . . .") His father this time. But in vain again. Or perhaps too late. For Larry had strained and strained toward a sky, where, especially for him it seemed, all the stars remained forever still.

Just ahead of them walked Tessa with Marco. Marco, his arm about Tessa's waist, his face bent toward her ear. He wore no talisman: his Moroccan hand was nowhere in sight. He held Tessa quite close. Her mother, when she turned around, appeared quite unconcerned. She was enjoying herself, especially since she had acquired the guide. She looked up; she looked down; she looked into the distance; she looked all around; she asked questions; she pointed something out to Francesco, who was dragging his feet.

Larry knew exactly how Tessa's brown waist must feel. Bare and warm, cooled off at times by the wind that blew in slight gusts, sideways, like a draft among the ruins. Tessa's waist, with that particular smell of slightly singed skin, oil of Coppertone, and the men's cologne she used. (No

perfume ever, Tessa knew, under the light of the sun; because of the essence of bergamot, it could leave ugly and
persistent brown stains on the skin.)

Naked, that waist. Lazy, her walk. And although she
had modestly wrapped a length of Polynesian cotton about
her hips, the top of her was bare except for the token bra,
several rows of seashells, and a fistful of gold rings. If only
Theodora would stop her lessons about the broken stones.
For a time, she was silent. Larry looked at her. She was
upset all of a sudden; as if she had forgotten or lost something
important.

"Do you know what we've missed?" she asked.

"No," answered Larry.

"The Agora of the Italians."

"Yes?" Larry asked politely.

"I think it's the largest monument on Delos. It was enormous. I can see a restored portico from here, way over there
by the Sacred Lake."

(Again, she pointed far off — in the general direction of
the lions.)

Silently, Larry walked on.

"*Agora* means 'marketplace,'" said Theodora. "Or else
a place of assembly." She halted; she seemed a little out of
breath. "It must have been perfectly beautiful. So spacious
that each side was lined with a row of shops. Can you imagine? And inside, huge votive statues and columns, mosaics,
and — balconies, and crowds. Oh, how I wish I could have
been there. Italians, you see, made up the single largest
population on Delos. The place was simply crawling with
them — "

Larry walked on.

"Shall we tell them about it?" Theodora asked brusquely.

"No, no," he hastily stopped her. And then, treacherously, confidentially for the first time; "Haven't you noticed? They're not *really* interested. I don't know why they came in the first place."

"You're right, of course; you're absolutely right."

They visited the House of Trident. It was nautical, for the most part: one mosaic floor had an anchor with a dolphin wound about it; another, a beribboned trident; and a third, a perfectly shaped and justly famous, strangely three-dimensional amphora that Larry knew his mother — had she been with them — would have wanted to lift off the ground, smuggle home, and reassemble on the Spanish refectory table in the drawing room. It was while they were looking at the vase that Theodora absently said: "I think a Doric column has twenty-two sides to it, don't you?"

They saw a reservoir that was like a long rectangular swimming pool, in which a large healthy fig tree grew.

They saw an aqueduct.

"Must be Roman," said Larry.

By the aqueduct, Tessa's mother opened her bag again and gave the guide another coin, very graciously; he tipped his cap, took leave of them with a *"Ciao"* and an *"Adio,"* scaled a low wall, and promptly disappeared into the wilderness.

With a half-apologetic gesture and a smile, Tessa's mother pointed the way to Theodora, who hesitated for a second before she said: "Right then. To the theater!"

It was a call to battle. (Agincourt!) And so — they all went to the theater.

Larry was excited at the prospect, but as soon as they came upon it, he was terribly disappointed and must have looked it, because Theodora said, "Don't worry. Even the guide book dismisses it by saying it's pretty dilapidated."

"Seated five thousand once," Theodora said, and sat down on the relic of a seat. She looked exhausted.

"Let's rest a bit," she said.

The stones of the theater were strangely stained with spots of rust, and the moss that grew on them was rusty too.

Larry saw Tessa's mother, walking onstage all by herself, as in a dream. Tessa sat down and Sandro took out his Minox.

Click, click, click, went the tiny camera.

Larry watched them until Theodora said to him, "You know, my dear Lawrence, I was testing you, back on the beach this morning. It was innocent enough, particularly because I thought I'd never see you again."

She looked at him sideways, then up at the sky, where she found a fuzzy, thin, white crescent of a moon, rising.

"And so," she said, and paused. "We have gone to the moon."

Larry was silent. He had no idea what the woman was getting at. Nor, apparently, did she.

"I feel all over the place today," she finally said. "Too much travel."

And, after another pause: "What I really wanted to find out this morning was whether or not you were a true child of the coming decade. In a way, I was glad to see that you were not. Not really. A maverick, perhaps . . . (a word I dislike)."

Larry knew the word. He had seen it in print, but he had never heard it spoken.

"Causes," Theodora said, and folded her arms. "Causes," she repeated, and crossed her legs. "They're the real bedmates of the young today. Sixteen years old and preparing their revolution. Going off to sleep worried sick over the treatment of this or that minority. Now I'm being simplistic,

I know, and on purpose. But my daughter's not like that (through some geographical accident, perhaps). Nor are you. Nor is our little group over there, I'm happy to say. Hedonists, all of them. Honest sun worshipers with no pretensions. And meantime, back on his Vatican balcony, stands their latest link to old Apollo. You should see him, my dear, giving every single blessed person in the crowd below his undivided attention. As if each one of them had not already made his own arrangements with the Above; the very same ones, I assure you, that his ancestors had, back in the Italian Agora."

She continued on a thoughtful note, and joined to it a thoughtful stare, "Promise me that you'll live a little before you start existing for causes. They'll catch up with you in time. The classical bit, you know, like death — "

Larry, who knew the end of that sentence, allowed himself to interrupt.

"But what shall I do?"

"Observe!" she said grandly, with a panoramic gesture of the right hand that was far *too* grand not to be slightly ridiculous.

"Look around. Watch. Listen carefully. Watch those Italians over there. Live. I don't know whether or not it works for them, but try it. Live as hard and as fully as you can."

So, I must watch broken columns and live hard while I do this, Larry thought. I must listen carefully to *bouzouki*, but for once there is none. Thank God. I must observe. I must observe Tessa. And the others. And it's exactly what I *have* been doing since the second of August. Does this mean that I have learned to live fully and correctly?

He wasn't sure, because in a way Theodora had tricked him. Where was the demarcation line between living and existing? Did he merely *exist* at Madame Duperrex' side and *live* when he was in Tessa's proximity? Could Madame Duperrex and her two dunces come anywhere near being called a *cause?* They certainly came under the heading of duty. And what was he up to at that very moment? Was he living fully, his eyes held by Theodora's hand, waving in the direction of a faraway column that stood all by itself, apparently intact with its capital on, against that relentless blue?

(". . . the most glorious monument to Isadora is a handful of photographs of her taken by Genthe at the Parthenon. One particularly: arms raised, each resting on a column; her head thrown back; and those long draperies. Superb. Absolutely superb . . .")

Larry had heard the sound of his mother's voice so clearly in his mind that he wondered whether, without being aware of it, he missed her actual presence. He thought not. It was habit, that was all: that voice to him was simply the most familiar one of them all. But he couldn't imagine why he had the capacity to retain all those meaningless proper names. He turned around, looking for Tessa, but Theodora recalled him.

"You know, I think that regime is here to stay. And there's very little you or I or anybody else can do about it. Even staying away won't *really* help. It's a stand, I'll admit. But the tourists are flocking, to coin a phrase. Actually, staying away *can* be a pose. Are you musical?"

"No, not really."

"Take Casals. He finally gave in: couldn't bear to miss the White House, from what I hear."

Larry had never heard of Casals and was not about to ask who he was. (But would he, in spite of himself, retain that name too?) In any case, he didn't have a chance. Theodora had been launched.

"Everything in Greece looks flimsy, doesn't it? Including that baby blue wooden entrance to the pier on the island with that stupid bird on top. Well, so do the chalets in the mountains near Zurich. And yet most of them have been standing for hundreds of years in a very harsh climate and without the help of a single nail. I don't seem to know what I'm talking about anymore. Certainly my analogy makes little sense. Come on, let's all go." (Looking at her watch.) "I still have to get on that boat for Athens tonight."

She rose.

Larry saw Tessa's mother walking toward them. To Theodora, she said: "I think it would be good if we went back to the boat; the sailor — "

"My God, yes," said Theodora, as if the idea had only just occurred to her, "let's by all means go."

They all walked, close together now, in the direction of the port, and Larry began to doubt that he would ever be able to make his way off this island and on to another one.

For he had much ahead of him. The boat trip back. At least half an hour's walk uphill, in the dark, in the dust, like a donkey. Arrive at the Duperrex' rented house — "villa," as Madame Duperrex liked to call it. Open squeaky garden door. Down the tall uneven steps. No light. Stumble. Yellowish lights on, above Jean-Marc's and Daniel-Georges' bunks, the door to their room left wide open. The nightly mosquito hunt. (Was that living fully?) Floor littered with the shells of pistachio nuts. Pangs of hunger. Would he be fed? Before he passed out? Goat cheese and olives, if he was lucky. Jean-Marc throws *Astérix et Cléopatre* at Daniel-Georges. The binding flies off and they begin a noisy fight. And then Madame Duperrex' voice, from another part of the house: "C'est toi, Larry?"

He felt very sorry for himself.

"Stop!" shouted Theodora. He did. "Now you can see them. They're marvelous from here. Look! Look at the lions!"

And Larry was a small boy again, with his mother at the London Zoo. He vividly remembered the sign in the shape of an arrow that pointed TO LIONS AND TEA. And his mother bent sideways toward him, her head up, cropped hair shining, explaining to him the lion asleep in his cage. Tea was even better. There were two: plain tea and children's tea. Children's tea was a chimpanzee tea party. Four chimpanzees, sitting at a table all dressed up with bibs, and his mother, saying: "Aren't their manners splendid?" just before the tin cups flew.

The light was so clear and deceptive that he had long ago given up judging, or misjudging, distances.

"There are five now; originally there were nine." (Pause.) "Five were found on the site. One is now in Venice — the *vandals.*"

Larry had not yet formed an opinion as to what should remain in place and what could be carted away, if anything. He simply had never given it a thought.

"They're terribly old and made of Naxos marble," Theodora said, without the help of the *Guide Bleu.* "They really *are* splendid. But of course you've already seen them — on all the postcards," she said regretfully.

And it was true that he had. Much closer up, too.

" 'Noble animals, they turn their backsides to the sea' — or was it 'their backs to the seaside'?" She laughed. "I can't remember. From some stupid translated guide book; not the blue one," she loyally added.

Sandro ran up to Tessa and took her arm. She pouted, disengaged herself, and moved on. But a moment later she let him move up to her; now she took *his* arm and leaned against it, and Sandro turned his face toward her. It was grateful, beatific, and dumb.

Her mother walked behind her, talking to Francesco, because Francesco looked more glum than he had ever looked before. He had pulled up his tight long bathing trunks that needed no pulling. He had run his hand through his hair that needed no combing. He looked up for a moment, and Larry found himself in the direct line of two familiar, familial eyes. They were glacial and Larry shivered, as if he had just had a bad premonition. Or else it was the wind, the penetrating wind, growing colder now as they came nearer to the port.

Marco had a primitive, swingy walk, quite heavy for someone so young, but he *was* big and tall. He was edging his way toward Tessa. Francesco walked with his head bent forward. His mother turned to Larry. "It was so *lovely*; don't you think?" (Her *o* as in lore.)

The boy flushed. "Yes," he said, and hesitated. "Very lovely," he said. He almost said, "Thank you," but stopped himself in time. He turned to Theodora.

"Would you like to walk in front of me?"

"No, this is splendid," she boomed.

But suddenly she was beside him. "We'll just make it in time; look at that sun. And to think that I'm off to Zurich in the morning — perfectly grotesque."

She walked close to him, and every once in a while it occurred to him that they must look ridiculous together; but he also felt that only he could understand the kind, stained smile, the lyrical voice, the delicate patterns on the roseate skin of the cheek that was turned toward him, the eager eyes, reddened by sunlight and lack of sleep. For he was certain that, unlike Madame Duperrex, she was not one to indulge herself. The way she poured, like an alchemist, enthusiasm into kindness, and kindness back into enthusiasm. How pretty she might have been once — forty, no, perhaps thirty years ago.

They walked through a house and Larry saw Tessa stoop way down on her haunches and, with a long fingernail, pry off a small stone from the very edge of a mosaic floor. It came out quite easily. She straightened, opened her mouth, and for a moment held it between her front teeth, while she adjusted her length of Polynesian cotton. It was a square piece of grayish marble, thousands of years old, that looked like dirty candy, which she dropped into her bra. But her breast was so small and so neat that the stone stuck out lamentably. This she realized, so she took it out again, and just kept it in her right hand, and toyed with it.

"It is strictly forbidden to . . ."

"*Defense de* . . ."

And the Italian.

And the German.

And the Greek.

Which Larry could certainly not reconstruct, particularly as he had not the slightest notion of the Cyrillic alphabet. Everybody saw what Tessa had done, but nobody said anything. Larry decided he must be altogether too law-abiding.

On they walked, held together now by what they had shared: desolation, beauty, fatigue, hunger (was that shared or mostly Larry's?), and the almost voyeuristic aspect of moving from house to house — a sort of desecration, so different from a visit to a museum, in spite of the fact that they were no longer houses at all.

It was twenty to seven, and Larry was cold. Marco and Tessa walked silently, hand in hand. Francesco was with his mother. Marisa and Sandro led the way, slightly bent toward each other.

Marco whispered something in Tessa's ear, and she laughed again. Then he kissed the lobe of that ear. He put his arm around her waist. She hesitated, then reciprocated.

If only I were Italian, Larry thought. Then I might be in a position to do something. At least I would be in the running; in spite of the fact that Marco is so much older than I am.

"Le marché de Délos était abondamment fourni en esclaves," Theodora read from her *Guide Bleu.*

She stopped for a moment and sighed. She looked at Larry and smiled her sad smile. They were old friends. She looked very tired.

I shall never be anything more than Tessa's silent slave, Larry thought (for he was an old-fashioned boy who went to an old-fashioned school).

Francesco turned to his mother. He looked ravaged. He always did when he was tired; only this time it was more than fatigue. Something had happened. Francesco spoke to his mother, and when he raised his voice slightly, Larry heard the name Marco, delivered with a good deal of malevolence. Marco obviously heard him, for he turned around, looked at him, smiled very briefly, and continued on his way.

Francesco's mother took his arm, as if she needed assistance. It was a gesture of unexpected tenderness.

"See that?" Theodora asked. "Over there?" She pointed across the water. "That's Reneia, or Big Delos."

She no longer read.

"Nothing there," she said. "But it once served both as a cemetery and a birthplace for Delos. It was sacred then — to Apollo (he was born here, you know) — then someone, can't remember who, decided to purify it; so he decreed that no one was to die, or be born, on Delos."

She passed the back of her hand across her forehead. "I'm perfectly exhausted."

She tried to smooth her hair again. It was hennaed, her only attempt at cosmetics, but between the sun, the salt water, her travels, the wind, and her present state of fatigue, there was nothing constructive to be done with it at the moment.

"Did you know that?"

He shook his head back and forth, the non-Greek way.

"I didn't think you would. Well, the women about to give birth and the people about to die were transported to Big Delos express. There must have been some emergencies, but none recorded in the history books."

Larry saw, suddenly, a miniature railroad track with an empty wagon on it. It looked so strange, like a mislaid toy, in the wilderness by the sea.

"Who's digging?" he asked.

"The French," Theodora answered. "Look at that cistern over there — super water system."

The wooden booth by the dock was deserted. The two soldiers had obviously known Karalombo (and the two Frenchwomen?). Perhaps Karalombo had told the soldiers that his clients were perfectly reliable, and so they had gone off for Greek coffee. But where? To the new stucco houses, perhaps. At any rate, the booth was closed.

And so any one of them could have taken off with a large vat for olive oil, an amphora, or a lovely piece of numbered column, and nobody would have been the wiser. Vocal persuasion, a strong handshake, a good bribe to seal his promise of silence; then a simultaneous gold-and-enamel smile from Karalombo. Larry was certain it could be done. Tessa's stone. The world was corrupt. The only difference (and possibility) lay in size and weight. Those vats were not only too large but unspeakably heavy. Perhaps those two factors alone substituted relative safety for honor. Honor never sufficed in the face of temptation. It was the degree of temptation that counted. And it wasn't until Larry had set foot on Delos that he had felt, for the first time, the wish to hold in his hand an object — anything at all — that was several thousands of years old. He had therefore understood the meaning of pillage.

His mother kept three minute stones, one copper red, one white, another a deep blue-green, together with several loose pearls and two large and veined turquoise beads, in an envelope at the bottom of her jewel box. Once Larry had seen her finger them dreamily and, still a small boy, he had asked: "What is that?"

"Oh, nothing," his mother had said, and paused. "From the Ravenna mosaics. Just a keepsake." And she had dropped them back (drop — drop — drop), her thoughts very far away, and the envelope had folded over them automatically, and Larry knew, even then, that she had told him neither the beginning nor the end of that story, and that she never would.

So that now, he suddenly caught himself stalking, with lowered eyes, the broken stone with the two petals of a rose design on it, the palm of a hand without its fingers, or, miracle of miracles, a small enough, almost intact head of a horse, which must lie there somewhere behind that stone — the overnight cache of an excavator who had prepared his next day's coup.

"I hope that you are not too cold." (Tessa's mother.)

"No, no," Larry answered gratefully. He wished he had a windbreaker. The meltémi had risen again. They now stood on the dock.

Karalombo and Sandro were busy with the thick rope that

slipped through Karalombo's hands like a highly malleable domesticated snake. The sailor shouted orders to Sandro in Greek. Eloquent mime took care of Sandro's hesitations. They worked fast.

The sun, a deep burnt orange and full, but already neatly cut off at the bottom, had begun a majestic splashdown. (Larry's imagery, these days, was inevitable.)

XVII

Francesco helped his mother on board, then Marisa, then Tessa. He did not look after Theodora because she still stood there riveted by the sunset. Marco had disappeared. Theodora finally turned toward the boat, and so Francesco helped her on. His manner was deferential. Francesco and Larry scrambled on more or less together; the sailor urged them on. Marco came running; Karalombo was not pleased with him.

Tessa's mother had arranged herself in the central, covered part of the caïque. Larry suddenly decided that it was laid out like a church. The benches were narrow and hard. The sailor's cabin, at the prow, substituted for an altar.

Larry did not know why this idea had come to him. None of them had seemed particularly moved by the religious aspect of a visit to sacred Delos, except perhaps for Theodora. But now a strange hush fell over them all. Karalombo jumped into the boat, counted his passengers, and ran into his cabin. The door banged twice behind him, inaudibly, because of the overpowering sound of the motor that soon rocked them all into further silence.

Marco sat in the wind on the bench that rimmed the caïque. It could easily have held fifty, sitting in the oval, and he looked very much alone.

Tessa pulled on a heavy sweater. She had, at the moment, not quite made her way through it; she was having trouble fitting the neckline over her head. Her mother already wore a cardigan. Theodora had put hers on at the dock.

Larry watched them, remembering Theodora's advice ("Observe!"), and recorded nothing. Until the idea came to him — very simply, just like that — that in a few minutes, past those rocks over there, something terrible would happen.

A wave would wash over the caïque and it would overturn, like a tiny sailboat. No, it wouldn't. One, two waves would cover it in close succession, two immense waves that would move in unheralded from the eye of a storm farther out at sea and wash most of them overboard.

He was suddenly terrified of being hit by the side of the overturned boat, or of being trapped under it. He did not fear so much the open sea. He would forget Tessa's mother, and rescue her daughter. (Was it not a rule of the sea? Had not the mother lived out most of her life, that life Theodora liked to speculate about?) Tessa had only just begun hers. And she would cling to him with all her strength, which was not to be underestimated. Larry closed his eyes. A wave washed over him; he did not let go. He could survive; *they* could survive, he did not doubt, until help came. (Ah, but *when* would it come? This was Greece, remember . . .)

Theodora tapped him on the shoulder.

"Not too tired?" she shouted in his ear.

He felt dead.

Larry tried to concentrate on the caïque's majestic trajectory (an ample arc) out of the port and on the finality of the sunset. Would the sun rise in the morning? I must stop that immediately, he thought, consoled by the fact that he wasn't the first to whom that idea had occurred.

"You must be hungry," Theodora shouted in his ear. She

was obviously well acquainted with the needs of growing boys. Low blood sugar, that's all it was; his doctor had explained it to him. But he did not feel the least little bit hungry anymore; only low, as if his soul was in decline. He could see how starvation would eventually (quite soon, in fact) bring on delusion.

"I'm very well," he shouted back in Theodora's ear. "Very grateful," he added, and flushed.

Theodora nodded her head. Her pleasure with him was obvious.

Francesco moved about: uncertain, sullen, difficult, inaccessible, incomprehensible. As if the only thing he wanted the world to realize was that sundown was not his time of day, and let no one come anywhere near him, please.

But then, a moment later, Sandro went up to him, to ask a question that Francesco answered affably enough, and Larry decided that he had not measured the situation correctly. It was not so easy, with Italians. He wasn't used to them yet, that was all.

Thirty, thirty-five minutes more, and the island would slowly rise from the dark, like a sleeping gull.

The sea, on the return trip, was truly rough; much rougher than anything Larry had expected.

Marisa suddenly gave a yelp, high pitched, like a puppy's. And then, as the caïque settled, momentarily, she laughed. Sandro spoke to her, and she laughed again as he smoothed out her already smooth hair. She seemed comforted enough to say something to him, and then they both laughed.

The roar of the motor was louder returning than going. Larry didn't know why. Theodora smoked another Gauloise in total silence and concentration.

Marco's longish straight hair flew back directly from the neat line of his head. He had a heavy but extraordinarily pure profile. They were all beautiful, those Italians. They all had their moments, when one took over from the other, but they were all beautiful, there was no denying that.

Tessa turned to Larry, just as he was staring at her. She looked frankly tired: the full mouth, drawn at the corners; the chin, loosened and round; the eyes, painted, the neat lines blurred by the many hours that had passed since she had traced them. They appeared to become luminous at twilight; there was nothing much else, really, in that solid brown face at the moment. The eyes, their eyelashes blackened, the delicate skin under them purple dark.

Promptly, he lowered his.

Tessa knocked Marisa with her elbow — a lazy movement, — drew her near, and whispered something to her. No need to whisper, really. Larry knew, more or less, what it was all about. Marisa turned slightly and Larry felt the beginnings of a blush just as the boat gave such a sudden lurch that his stomach rose into his throat. Altogether, he had good reason to be grateful for the failing light.

Francesco moved carefully up and down the aisle, his hands grasping and leaving the backs of seats, as if he still needed to spend a certain amount of energy he no longer appeared to possess.

Marco came and sat next to Marisa. He looked stiff with cold.

The caïque's progress was now very slow. Larry braced himself and adjusted his mind to the prospect of an elongated and disagreeable half-hour (at least), just as he did when he saw the FASTEN YOUR SEAT BELTS sign light up in an airplane.

Theodora thoughtfully threw her cigarette overboard.

Larry wished he had some Marzine along for motion sickness. He only hoped to avoid the vomiting point. He did not really mind discomfort, but he was humiliated by the fact that he was not as sturdy a traveler as he would have liked to be. Oh God — he did not want Tessa to see him lunge around to vomit overboard. He sat very still.

To make matters worse, Karalombo rushed out of his cabin, looked about wildly in every possible direction, and then rushed in again. Behind him, the door banged twice. Then he must have closed it. Inexplicable. How could he leave the steering wheel unattended? Larry's stomach heaved.

Theodora said slowly: "I wish I hadn't smoked that Gauloise. Filthy tobacco!" Her voice was deeper and her delivery more quaky than before. After that, she fell silent again.

The Italians went into a huddle. Francesco stood slightly stooped over them, his hands firmly gripping the backs of two seats. He listened attentively to something his mother said, then he weaved his way very carefully up the center aisle toward the sailor's cabin. At certain moments, when progress became impossible, he simply stopped and waited.

Marisa, her face resolutely set, pulled back all of her hair with both her hands. She held the weight of it with her thumbs. Back went her head; up went her hair. She now held it in her left hand; with her right, she imprisoned it in an elastic. Now her right hand held it while the left tugged at the rubber band. She was getting herself ready for a cataclysm.

XVIII

Tessa. Oh, Tessa. Larry thought he must soon vomit. It was more than hours, it felt like days since he'd eaten. Marco said something to Marisa, who moved over. He now sat between the two girls. Soon he bent toward Tessa and put his arm around her. Her mother spoke to Sandro. Sandro had put a sailor's or a skier's knitted cap on his head. Francesco carefully made his way back to the center aisle. The cabin door banged only once before it shut.

Oh please, dear God, Larry prayed again to no one in particular, don't let me vomit.

Francesco sat down next to Sandro and bent over him in order to speak, very loud, to his mother.

Marco got up; so did Tessa. He held her right hand. There was nothing whatsoever on the horizon. It seemed impossible, but there it was or, rather, was not. Nothing but a very turbulent and dark sea with huge waves intermittently breaking. Tessa laughed after she lost her balance and almost fell, and Marco caught her. He held her for a moment, folded against him; after that, he just held her. Her arms stayed at her side, but she no longer smiled. She even closed her eyes. As if this was the time for that sort of thing.

This misery. I'm about to vomit, Larry thought, and turned his head slowly toward the sea.

"Bearing up?" Theodora asked.

He nodded. (Up and down, very slowly.)

Marco stepped back, gripped Tessa's left hand, and moved on, holding on to the polished backs of benches with his right. Tessa's mother shouted something at them, which Marco did not hear or else chose to ignore.

Tessa and Marco now sat a little forward on the bench that rimmed the caïque, halfway between Karalombo's cabin and the rest of the group.

What misery, Larry thought, as the boat lurched and his stomach heaved. Tessa's hair flew in the wind. Her eyes were wide open. There was something reckless in her that Larry had never seen before, had never even suspected; he had only known and loved her surfeited, aloof, and bored.

Francesco got up, changed his mind, and sat down again. Theodora said calmly, "This is awful, simply awful." Larry did not know what she meant by "awful." So many things were awful, all of a sudden. And he felt so helpless. And they were in actual, physical danger.

Larry wanted to ask Theodora, but was incapable of action. He didn't want either to allay or to share Theodora's fears, or even find out what she really wanted to say. He wanted to keep as quiet as possible; the only thing he could do, actually *do*, was to keep his eyes open, and observe and try not to vomit.

There was a long moment of pause, of silence, broken by the crash of waves against the hull of the boat.

Larry moved his head very carefully and saw an archipelago of pointy black rocks which the sea alternately revealed and almost effaced. So that was why Karalombo steered the caïque on an elliptical course that appeared to destine it for the open sea.

The sailor seemed to know what he was doing — well, he had to. He had never done anything else in his life, nor, probably, had his father.

Another wave crashed against the hull; the spray rose in a high, thin arc and fell onto the forward part of the open deck.

Tessa and Marco were drenched. Tessa had screamed, a pure and joyous scream, and Marco had smoothly taken her into his arms and still they did not seek shelter. And no one said anything. They sat on the hard bench, intertwined, now against sea, now against sky.

Larry turned to Theodora, more suddenly than he would have wished. His skin was all in goose pimples. He felt wretched. He felt frozen and alone. Theodora moved her kind, gray eyes from Marco, to Tessa, to her mother, and

back to the couple again. Tessa's mother sat with her usual
calm, but with an unusual rigid dignity, strained arms
crossed over her lap, hands cupped on the outside of her
knees. Francesco spoke to her; she lifted her right hand
and placed it on his shoulder. She said nothing. She looked
infinitely sad and totally unmoved by any sense of danger.
Francesco stood by his mother, his back to Marco and
Tessa. He stood straight for once, his mother held in safety
by his half-extended arms and hands that gripped both the
back of the bench she sat on and the one in front of her.
Larry could see the long line of tension that extended from
his collarbone into his shoulders, down his arms, and into
his hands. The fingers, extended against the back of the
benches, had very white fingernails. Perhaps it was the cold,
or the wind, or both.

Theodora shuddered; then she said to Larry, "It's been
a very long day." (Pause.) "I almost wish it were over."

Marisa shouted at Francesco, and he sat down again.
Sandro slid up to Marisa, and their heads moved alternately,
depending on who spoke and who listened.

Larry could see the outline of Tessa's head and the back
of Marco's, his face buried in Tessa's neck. The dark head
of hair moved very gently as he kissed her once, and then
once again.

Francesco stood up. His mother, this time, gave him a
sharp command, and he sat down on the very edge of his
seat.

"Really!" said Theodora. But she sounded neither shocked
nor unkind. (It seemed that this was the thing to say,
under the circumstances, and so she had said it.)

"Observe," she had told Larry, and observe he did. But
he couldn't, for the life of him, understand what was happening. Theodora obviously had some sort of insight into

the situation. It mattered little; he felt much too queasy, at the moment, to ask or say anything.

He would question Theodora later; on the docks perhaps, before they parted, probably forever.

Would Tessa, chastened and aloof, be back on the beach tomorrow? Would he speak to her? Would she speak to him? Would he still love her? Did he love her now? Would he, eventually, have to vomit in spite of all his efforts not to?

So far so good. He thought he might make it. A slight imbalance of the inner ear, that's all it was. Sometimes age took care of it. After all, he did seem to improve with every trip.

(". . . traveling with Larry used to be a calvary; I had to change from head to foot before I could face a *chasseur* . . .") His mother, of course.

Tessa in Marco's arms. Just like that, in front of her mother and everyone else. How strange. How strangely unpleasant.

He wanted to look elsewhere and did automatically, when Tessa's mother said something to Francesco that made him get up, resolutely this time.

He walked toward Marco and his sister, but his progress was perilous and slow.

"Oh, my. I just wonder," said Theodora, very loud in her quaking contralto. And she bent over to pick up the watermelon bag that lay shapeless at her feet in order to get another cigarette. So that she missed the opening entirely.

It was Marco who hit first. Francesco fell back, but not far. He landed against the profile of a bench, and it stopped him.

Tessa screamed, a neat, expected scream. Francesco, stooped for better balance, his feet apart, moved forward again. Marco looked right, then left, for a quick way to elude him, saw that there was none, and gathered his legs under him so that he now crouched on the bench that rimmed the caïque.

The boat lurched again. Francesco stumbled forward, aimed incorrectly, and hit air. He barely missed Tessa, who threw herself aside and screamed once more, neither as loud nor as simply as the first time.

Larry ran and kneeled on the bench, his face to the sea, in order to be able to vomit overboard if it came to that. He was covered in sweat, yet the wind was bitingly cold. The water looked extremely turbulent, almost black. Nothing happened.

So he turned around, his back to the sea. Arms outstretched, he held on to the railing.

Marco unwound slowly. Now he stood almost full length on the bench, so that when Francesco managed to climb on, on the other side of Tessa, and hit him very hard and fast against the side of his head, he simply lost his balance and fell over the side in an unexpectedly dark and silent arc.

They all heard the splash over the sound of the motor. Francesco jumped down off the bench. Tessa screamed, this time like a heroine of the silent screen, her fists against her cheeks: no sound came out of her.

"Go! Go!" Theodora shouted at Larry.

But Sandro was already on his way to Karalombo's cabin.

Everyone moved, except for Francesco. Everything happened terribly fast.

Karalombo ran out of his cabin; Sandro pointed; Karalombo looked overboard and shouted a very loud oath in Greek that Larry did not understand. But the meaning was clear. He then slapped his thighs (very *plié*) with the palms of his hands, hard, and ran back into the cabin. Its door was left open and it banged, and banged again, and banged once more.

They all stood up at the railing, except for Tessa and her mother, who had somehow found each other. Her mother held her firmly. Tessa's shoulders moved up and down, very hard, but still no sound came out of her. (Larry would have preferred the most piteous screams.)

The caïque began an almost unbearably slow and arduous maneuver. Marisa screeched something at Sandro; and in the way of an answer, Sandro hit her on the shoulder with his hand. Marisa shut up, and hugged her smarting shoulder.

Below, in the very heavy sea, Marco's head appeared. It was more sleek and more wet, somehow, than any swimmer's head had any right to be. He no longer looked like a swimmer; he looked like a castaway. His mouth was wide open. Now he looked like a fish.

Larry wondered what he could do. Francesco hoisted himself up on the bench, looked into the sea, and stepped down again.

Down below, Marco opened and closed his mouth. Night fell slowly. Slowly, the boat began to turn around. Tessa still sobbed silently. Her mother still held her.

A tall wave completely erased Marco for a long moment, and Larry got ready to jump overboard. He was, after all, a very strong swimmer. But Theodora gripped him firmly by the shoulder. Marco reappeared, his face obliterated by the soaking hair that clung to it; but he managed to shake his head and even shake his hair back. His mouth opened again, and closed.

Theodora shouted in Larry's ear: "Don't worry; we'll soon pick him up."

Another tall wave washed over Marco and swallowed him.

There was a sharp intake of breath from Larry, almost a moan, as he waited for the head below to reappear. But it did not.

Larry watched the empty surface of the sea: the next wave, and the next. He watched Karalombo throw a bright orange life jacket overboard, and it fell exactly where it should have fallen. But even before that happened, Larry knew it was too late. He knew it was the end.

Sophia, Zoltan, and the Postman

All the people in our circle — brokers, shopkeepers, clerks in banks and steamship offices — taught their children music. Our fathers, unable to see any other way out, had devised a lottery, and organized it on the flesh and bones of their little ones. Odessa more than other towns was seized by this madness.

— From *Tales of Odessa* by Isaac Babel.

ON A RAINY SPRING DAY IN PARIS, in the year 1939, the postman climbed the six floors to Sophia's garret, cursing all the while, and knocked on her door. It was ajar and there was no answer. Holding a letter from Zoltan, he walked in and found Sophia thrown back against her four fat pillows, dead.

In the darkened room, the postman stood, sopping wet and still, hit by visions of his own mortality. (He was fifty-eight; Madame Sophie, as he called her, had been sixty.) She had so often threatened him from her bed, with the broken umbrella that still stood propped up against her night table, but a puddle on the carpet no longer mattered. He noted an open telegram on the floor, by the umbrella. He saw that she looked quite placid, and not unusually pale. It was the fear of finding her still warm that kept him from going up to touch her. When had it happened? Stupidly, he began to cry. She had come to Paris — when was it? About forty years ago? He had hated her because she spoke such execrable French — a real Russian savage. But they had also been friends. Every morning (except Sundays and holidays and the winter he went down to Morocco to get over his chronic bronchitis) they had shared a moment of communication so intense it bordered on thought transmission. Was there, today, a letter from Zoltan? And, in later years, was there, perhaps, a letter from Bobka? The postman started to return the letter to his wooden box, but instead, hesitantly, he put it on her night table. Then he nodded several times, blew his nose into a checked handkerchief, and started down the stairs in search of the concierge.

*

There had been nothing unusual about Sophia's last morning on earth. She awakened with the customary prickly pains in the joints of her legs — the right one especially — and the pains took off, to ride turbulently up and down the lengths of her limbs until she felt her blood turn to seltzer water. And she had the usual trouble raising herself, because she had been getting fat lately, like an unclaimed pearl feeding on nacreous walls in the darkness. Undulating slowly, she rubbed her back against her pillows. "Dai, dai, de-rai, dai, dai, dai, dai ——" she sang, to the tune of a waltz from *The Gypsy Baron*, "dai, dai, de-rai, dai, dai, de-rai . . ." And at the end of the phrase her right hand, with the two rings from Zoltan (the wide wedding band and the other, thin gold with two small diamond hearts) clasping the swollen flesh of her finger, reached for one of the many porcelain boxes on her bedside table. After removing the cover by its porcelain acorn, she picked out a large sunflower seed. She cracked it open with her false front teeth, chewed awhile, and, finally, spat the shells into a pin tray with a loud "tfoo!" Without bothering to open the shutters, she began to join a narrow strip of lace to the edge of a new pink pillowcase. She sewed slowly because her fingers were stiff, and all the time she was thinking of her husband, Zoltan, in Odessa, and of the mail, so unpredictable since the Bolsheviks had come, and of her son, Bobka, in New York, and and of how unpredictable he was. The next time she reached for a sunflower seed, she suddenly said aloud, "Today I shall have a letter from Zoltan."

＊

Zoltan was not his real name; he was born Isidor Abramovitch Strimmer. His father, the head of a barley export-import business in Odessa, was the boastful owner of ten trucks and forty men. Ten days after the birth of Isidor, his mother died, leaving his father, Abram, with four young children and a wish to keep her artist's soul on earth, because she had deciphered Rubinstein's Romances on a straight-backed piano that was never undressed of its Persian shawl, and read poetry in bed — occupations Abram admired and did not understand. On her deathbed she said, "Never forget that life without art for me is like soup without barley for you." And a few minutes later she had died. Abram, bereft, now longed for art to descend on his household, and bring glory with it, as it had, implacably, on several families of his acquaintance. Although music put him to sleep, he expected talent to ignite one of his children with a fulgurating wand that would release melody like fireworks, because in Odessa the shortest paths to glory had already been discovered; they were five parallel lines, and together they added up to a bar of music. But talent was necessary. For Abram, orthodox religion no longer existed. The bonds of piety had perhaps been shattered by the previous generation when it moved from a small village in Lithuania to New Street in Odessa; Abram had never inquired. But he longed to be released a little from his eternal dealings with the material world. He was not looking for financial improvement; therefore his motives were pure. He would have music, he would have glory, and a little piece of his wife's soul would return to him. He brought a fiddle to the house, but none of the children would come near it. According to his musical hierarchy, to earn a living by blowing into an instrument was a disgrace, to be a fiddler was respectable, to be a singer was illustrious. Attentively, he watched Isidor, an unexplained child because his eyes were dark yellow, his hair was red, his skin translucent, his neck overgrown. Isidor seemed to have an ear. Soon he developed a small true voice.

As Isidor grew conscious of his destiny as an opera singer, he secretly chose to call himself Zoltan. The name, for him, combined Boris Godunov and the Young Prince in the *Scheherazade* suite into a being of supreme power and temperament, who reigned over the beauties of Ingres's *Bath* (he had found a reproduction among his father's secret papers), and who sank regular teeth into greenish squares of hashish, which he swallowed like so much mint candy.

Zoltan, having grown his first red mustache, stood in a balletic fourth position in front of his assembled family and made the following announcement: "I will never be able to sing *Boris Godunov* under the name of Isidor Abramovitch

Strimmer. From now on, call me simply Zoltan." Under
that name he finished his studies at the St. Petersburg Con-
servatory.

❋

Zoltan met Sophia at a ball in Odessa. He was not impressed. Later that same evening, he described her to
friends as a case of cholera all dressed up in blue net. "The
only way I could tell her front," he said, "was by locating
the brooch." Actually, Sophia was recovering from typhus;
her hair had been cut very close to her head, and this elim-
inated most of its red reflection. Her longish nose occupied
most of her profile, and she had put herself out of the running altogether by allowing her chest to go flat. (Certain
Odessites who read Tolstoy never tired of discussing Karenin's ears and the merits of Anna's bosom, so full and perfect
that it jutted straight out like a tray, and how Anna, if she
had so chosen, could have balanced a tea service on it.)
Sophia had finished a course in midwifery at the University
of St. Petersburg, and had now begun to practice.

A week after the ball, Zoltan found her sitting on a bench
in Alexandrovsky Park, a heavy carpetbag beside her. The
bag was filled with pots, brochures, towels, and sterilizing
instruments. She had just helped deliver a friend's baby,
and was resting her feet on the way home. Sophia looked
better. She laughed, and showed off unusually good teeth
as she told Zoltan, "That infant, the only good thing one can
say about it is that it was alive, but Mania thought it
beautiful enough to exhibit in a store window on Richelieu
Street." Zoltan noted — with admiration — the modernity
of this young woman, as well as her blush, which was of an
extraordinary pink, almost orchid.

Zoltan proposed three weeks after, but Sophia could not

make up her mind. She wanted several sons and could not reconcile them with the trunks of Zoltan's future tours. But Zoltan, whom Sophia imagined to be a helpless romantic, an artist, a man with a golden throat held by a flowing tie, proved to be very enterprising. He bought a skeleton through a medical acquaintance, dismembered it into a suitcase, took the tramcar to the Dukovsky Garden, found a ruined grotto in which he had played as a child, and there, on the ground, carefully arranged the skull and a few bones. The following Sunday, he invited Sophia to a picnic, and somehow they found themselves at the mouth of his cave. Zoltan compared the immediate landscape to a set from *Hansel and Gretel*. Then he took off his fedora, bowed Sophia into the darkness. She heard him gasp as, with wild eyes, he pointed to the skull, and gasp again as he stumbled on a bone. "Sophia Isaakovna," he said, excessively rubato, "this is all that remains of someone who laughed, and cried . . . and loved. All that will be left of us someday — or perhaps suddenly, much sooner than we expect it — bones — " Encouraged by her silence, he kissed her narrow chin.

Two weeks later they were married. The year was 1900, and Sophia was twenty-one. As a wedding present, Zoltan's father gave them two years in Milan, where Zoltan could finish his studies. (Abram's pride in his son was immense. Soon he would have a full-grown artist in the family, instead of a run-of-the-mill *Wunderkind;* besides, he approved of the marriage.) As for Sophia, Milan long stood in her mind as a temple solely dedicated to the production of singers.

Exactly a year later, while Zoltan was trying out with a small Italian road company, Sophia gave birth to her first son, in their hotel room in Milan. "Oh, mother of mine!" she shouted in a lull. "You're killing me, I shan't live to see my son!" She screamed. (She had noted that only country maids had easy births.) She bit into her pillow, and tore the case in two. "My son," said Sophia as the midwife lifted the newborn, a mottled creature with uneven tufts of dark hair on its elongated head, and dark fur growing down its back. "My son is a prince." She called him Robert, for no reason in particular, and Robert became Bobka.

Meanwhile, Zoltan was in trouble. For the forty-eight hours preceding a performance he could swallow only liquids. He stared at a glass of tea, which he left to cool until it was too cold to drink; then he stared at the game of solitaire that he slowly shaped into an empty corner of his dressing table; finally, he stared once more at the glass of tea. He ate nothing, he drank little, and he sighed regularly like a spaniel. Nor was he able to leave his agitation in the dressing room. He dragged his fright onstage like so much refugee baggage, and it paralyzed him. He moved into place, an automaton with absent eyes; he stood in his balletic fourth position, his pink right hand against his chest; he inhaled evenly and slowly until his diaphragm, in profile, protruded in an extravagantly dangerous arc that intimidated the first row of the audience; then, at the very instant when the house was primed for a first note, from Zoltan's large, open mouth came — silence. After that, he was seen to waver evenly between one sandaled foot and the other, with an ever deeper roll, until, at last, still open-mouthed but now totally rigid, he fell on his side in a dead faint. He fainted once, he fainted twice; each time, he returned to Milan and his studies. Sophia laughed and said, "Never two without three!" But when Zoltan's father heard about a third fainting spell, he took to weeping in front of visitors and making resolutions and plans in private. He decided his son should apply himself to shipping barley, and Zoltan was recalled to Odessa. Terrified of the humiliations

his father no doubt held in readiness for him, Zoltan almost
wanted to die; he wanted to shed his duties, he wanted to
flee, he wanted to shed his skin. But first he reasoned that
he had no right to subject his wife and child to life with a
lowly employee, so he shed Sophia. He persuaded her to
join Rosa Iphimovna, her cousin, who lived in Paris.
Rosa — the elder by fifteen years — would take good care
of his wife and child; of that he was certain. Also, Rosa's
two daughters played the violin. One even studied at the
Conservatoire. Sophia would not be lost in the musical mi-
lieu. He promised to join her soon. He would take hold of
himself and continue his career; if he didn't, he would de-
vise, somehow, a business mission that would reunite them
in the near future.

*

Zoltan took a train for Odessa, and Sophia, with Bobka in
her arms, took a train for Paris, where she was met, in the
mist of the Gare de Lyon, by Rosa and her two daughters,
Manitchka and Zinotchka, both wearing bottle green velvet coats trimmed with red fox, and long, tight *Wunderkind* curls. Sophia moved into their capacious garret on the
Rue de La Fayette, and as soon as she had unpacked
her trunk, as soon as Bobka had gone to sleep on Rosa's bed
and the cabbage-and-chestnut soup heating on the spirit
lamp had been stirred, Sophia, without meaning to, began
to wait for a letter from Zoltan.

Bobka was never taken outdoors; instead, his basket was
set on the floor by an open window, next to the table on
which Sophia wrote her desolate letters. Bobka smiled when
the finished page flew above him toward the center of the
room, but Sophia liked to cry as she wrote, and smudge the
complaints with her index finger. Although she missed Zol-

tan's presence down to the slenderest detail (smell of his pockets on rainy days, as she had emptied them of tobacco specks), she felt at home. She helped Rosa with the cooking; Rosa cleaned and shopped and carried the shopping bags, ungrudgingly, to the sixth floor. But Sophia was constantly unnerved by the climate and the smell of that houseful of women living without men (all underwear touched by lavender sachets, and, in the bathroom, modest violet toilet water and oval cakes of jasmine soap).

Zoltan did not write.

The only mail from Odessa was sent by the husband Rosa had deserted, an Orthodox Jew, twenty-three years her senior, whom she detested with honesty and detachment, both of which Sophia found enviable. He sent Rosa a moderate allowance every three months, and so, in time, Sophia met the postman. The children grew. Manitchka read *Anna Karenina* in secret. She padded her chest, and each day Rosa took the cotton out. Zinotchka was doing well at the Conservatoire. Her right foot turned slightly inward, and she had a tendency to cry, or fall, at the slightest provocation. She was, of course, the more talented of the two. Everyone listened compassionately when Bobka began to sing. (He seemed to have an ear.) Sophia, resigned, introduced her nightgowns to lavender sachets.

※

When Bobka was three, Zoltan wrote a letter. Its style was untrammeled and its message unself-conscious; it was as if his first letter had followed a thousand others. He was well, and had just been transferred to accounts. Soon, he felt, he would have learned and earned enough to join her. And how was Bobka?

From that moment he wrote, sparsely. Sometimes he

included a money order. When he did, Sophia hung discreetly for a moment on the postman's neck and wept, tearing at her hair as soon as he had started down the stairs and she had ascertained the sum. She had come under the influence of Rosa, who had long since labeled all men pigs.

*

In 1909, when Bobka was eight, Zoltan came to Paris. He had grown more pink and florid; in fact, he had become enormous. He stood in the balletic fourth position and said, "I am now in the diamond business." He fell on his knee in Rosa's kitchen and handed Sophia two small diamond hearts. "Here," he said. "Make a ring." Then he sat down with Bobka on his lap, and his large hand measured the exact width of the child's chest. Zoltan felt how frightened his son was. "Don't you know me?" he said softly in Bobka's ear. "I am your father, come from Russia."

Zoltan brought a wicker trunk up to the sixth floor on his back and silently moved in. He never sang anymore. He conducted his business behind the locked door of their bedroom, to the accompaniment of international arguments. He was visited by young men with pale red beards, kaftans, and sometimes an acute pitch in their voices, and by older men, smooth-shaven, with astrakhan collars and buttons, and windpipes coated with *rahat-lokoum*. He carried his stones in his breast pocket, in carefully folded double envelopes of cream-colored paper and tissue paper. At times he harbored a cat's-eye in transit — khaki, shadowy, broken by a single, transient ray of light — or a pale pink ruby, and it was with these stones that he liked to play store with Bobka. He lifted them from their envelopes with Sophia's eyebrow tweezers, and placed them on a jeweler's scale. There would be a bargaining argument; then their transaction would be sealed with the ancient Roman hand-clasp (the hand of one person clasping the forearm of the other) that Zoltan had learned in St. Petersburg. Bobka always resold the stones to Sophia — at a rather vulgar profit — and she would return them to Zoltan after Bobka was asleep.

Although Zoltan was growing still larger physically, his world appeared to have shrunk. His love of detail had become that of a very young child, and as a result he seemed engaged in miniaturism; he did not use a magnifying glass to observe an exiguous diamond. Wherever he happened to sit or stand, he registered, with the naked eye, specks of dust on the furniture, and would bend to observe them more closely; and after he'd taken a good look, he would begin to blow on them attentively.

He played with Bobka a great deal, but he had very little to do with the grown members of the household. Sophia suffered in silence during the day and took to weeping in her sleep; her dreams took place against swampy landscapes, and she woke with wet cheeks.

Then all of a sudden and for no apparent reason, Zoltan acquired a miniature pinscher. Its ears and tail had recently been clipped; it was unbelievably small, nasty, and febrile; and its appetite was enormous. It was released after meals to clean up under the table, and its name was Carpet Sweeper. Zoltan squandered all his love on the new playmate. He walked the dog in the morning and walked again in the afternoon, with the dog under his right arm and Bobka holding his left hand. When they stopped in front of the Bourse, Zoltan always made a wide gesture with his right arm, and, pointing with the dog — who whined and scratched in panic — announced: "In there, men are killing each other. You must never forget that." And Bobka's spine stiffened as he imagined the guillotine.

When business was good, Zoltan brought home vast assortments of garlic sausage, Greek olives, and smoked fish. For Sophia he bought Indian shawls with paisley drawings, and when spring came, he never failed to hang a bunch of violets on the inside of Rosa's kitchen door on the day she prepared the weekly Russian meatballs. (Rosa revenged herself on him — she had not wanted him there in the first place — by inflating the meatballs with potato and bread crumbs.)

But business, although Zoltan did not speak of it, seemed bad of late. The household suspected that he was in debt. When he was not out walking, he sat and stared, sighing regularly.

One morning, when Zoltan was out for an unexplained and solitary walk, Sophia heard the dog whine. She went into their bedroom. His leash was attached to his master's bed, and he was scratching the air. On her pillow were one of Zoltan's cream-colored envelopes and a note. "I am going back to Russia," it said. "Look after Bobka." The envelope was marked "To my son" and contained a small, watery sapphire, which Sophia hid in the granulated-sugar bin. Then she took to her bed. Bobka was not allowed in the room, but Rosa attended her while she wept, tore at her hair, and bit into all four pillows. When sorrow overpowered her completely, Rosa gave her a little ether to sniff from a secret bottle. For three days, Rosa could not tell whether the dog was infecting Sophia with his grief or whether it was the other way round. On the fourth day, while Sophia was sleeping, the postman came with a money order from Rosa's husband, and Rosa gave the dog to the postman to give to his wife, who took it at dawn the next day to the dog pound, where she had a fight with the attendant.

As soon as Sophia sat up in bed, Rosa felt it her duty to tell her that Zoltan had embezzled four pure, good-sized diamonds and fled with them to Odessa. On his part it was a simple act; the stones were in transit and hardly belonged to anyone. He had caught hold of a luminous toy, hugged it to his heart, and fled in full daylight, with just enough consciousness to know that he must run.

❋

Six months after Zoltan's flight, Sophia, who had kept her pregnancy secret, gave birth, prematurely, to her second son. Rosa attended her in her labor, which lasted ten minutes. The baby unexpectedly lived for almost a week, and unexpectedly died, smothered in a blanket.

Sophia took in sewing; she sewed for certain French ladies who liked to call themselves patronesses, and at whose houses Manitchka and Zinotchka, dressed in black velvet on Thursday afternoons, had fiddled for years behind potted dwarf palms; she sewed for the lady members of The Fellows of Odessa; and she sewed for a small group of Russian ladies, who wore necklaces of gutta-percha, drew the length of their eyelids with kohl, and liked to drink their tea lying down.

❋

Sophia had little money but was singularly unhampered by pride. Dressed in Rosa's best puce silk, she regularly called on a distant cousin who had become a personage since her marriage to the archeologist Professor Marshak. "Vera," she said. "Vera dear, do you want me to get on my knees?" She pointed to the dark, elegiac marvels of mahogany, the inlaid screens, the Japanese prints, the sofas covered in lees-of-wine plush with matching fringes punctuated by small silk bullets. "How can you live in all this luxury?" she asked, and, digging into her shallow knowledge of classical statuary, she said, "All you're missing here is the Apollon Bendersky," meaning to say, "Apollon Belvederesky." "Do you realize," she continued, "that every day I have to take the garbage down? Really, you should choke on your food, when Bobka has to go without his steak." Vera left the room and came back with a fairly thick pile of bank notes. Sophia bagged the money and clicked the clasp of her reticule exultantly, like castanets. In parting from Vera, she kissed her squarely on the mouth, and immediately said, "Tfoo!" as she pointed to a bundle on the refectory table. Inside, swaddled in a remnant of silk from Vera's new print dress, lay the small mummy of an ancient crocodile, its jaws yawning — so said Professor Marshak — at a reflection of the moon on the Nile.

As she rode back to the Rue de La Fayette from her visits to the Marshaks' (which she called her excavations), Sophia meditated on Professor Marshak's dry and fading goatee, Vera's childlessness, the fiery mustaches of her absent Zoltan, and Bobka's latest feat.

Bobka had an *idée fixe:* bananas. He also loved to sing. Although untrained, his voice was so strong and so dewy that even when used indiscriminately (the louder the better) it never failed, on a good day, to bring tears to his own as well as his mother's eyes.

He was an excellent actor. When Sophia gave him an empty milk can and some change, he soon returned, his face wet with tears. A black cat had furtively crossed his path as he was coming out of the dairy, and bad luck had struck him on the spot; in his fright, he had dropped the can and the cover had flown off. When Sophia gave him some change and a clean towel, he walked over to Vera Marshak's, carefully dampened the towel, washed his hands and face, and ran all the way back home in order to reach the correct shade of apoplectic red that Sophia expected from a visit to the Turkish bath. In each case he saved the money. His savings all went toward matinees at the theater and twilight visits to the small circus on the Rue Rochechouart, which he frequented so regularly that the director allowed him a special first-row seat.

Bobka hardly studied. He walked to school in order to pocket the fare and when he was late, the teachers sent him home.

"Who's there, who's there?" Sophia shouted in answer to a well-known knock on the door.

"Postman with registered mail," said a tired man's voice, wheezy after miles of fog and rain.

"Come in, come in," cried Sophia. Rosa came out of the kitchen. Zinotchka stopped fiddling and opened the door of her room. Sophia opened the front door. It was Bobka. He scudded in under her arm, ran like a rat (inhumanly close to the ground) toward his tiny bedroom, and locked himself in. Sophia tried to knock the door down with Rosa's umbrella, screaming, "Bandit! Criminal! Son of your father! Go to the Devil's mother! You will be responsible for my early death!" Then she sat down and sobbed, while Rosa and Zinotchka looked at each other over her bowed back. And then Rosa said gratefully, "You should have had a daughter."

Bobka knew exactly when to come out of his room, and he reappeared with a new set of Armenian riddles.

"Mama, what's ten feet tall and has a cross on top?"

"I don't know, Bobka, what is it?"

"A nurse on horseback, Mama, what else?"

Sophia did not laugh.

"All right, Mama, what is it that you like to eat, that hangs from the ceiling, and is painted green?"

"I don't know, dear, what is it?"

"A herring, Mama, what else?"

"But, Bobka, why painted green?"

"So you wouldn't guess my riddle, Mama dear, why else?"

And Bobka got down on one knee, one hand on his thin chest, and promised Sophia a letter from Zoltan. Then he lifted his head, dilated his nostrils, and closed one eye; with his arms extended like a somnambulist's, he walked toward Sophia's bedroom, from which he soon returned, still chewing, with four empty banana skins that were permeated with the lavender of Sophia's sachets.

*

In 1913, Sophia got a registered letter from Zoltan; it was vague and languorous. He was singing again — this time with an amateur choral group. He had been told that Sophia had lost their second child, and he was sorry. His father had died, leaving him a small inheritance — much smaller than he had expected. He was nevertheless including a money order; he felt it his duty to contribute regularly toward Bobka's education. Sophia was delighted. She wept over the letter, kissed the money order, called everyone in, and, overcome, went to bed. Then she reread the letter, and into it she read another woman. The short sentence "I am well taken care of" had brought Sophia to this conclusion. She did not speak of it to anyone, but she screamed at everybody. When Zinotchka, who had been rereading Tolstoy for almost a decade, came up to her bed one evening and said, "Aunt Sophia, let us once more discuss Karenin's big ears," Sophia, because she had forgotten, for the moment, just who had been unfaithful to whom, shouted, "All men are pigs, including Karenin, and you must never forget that!" A few days later, the postman brought a letter to Rosa informing her of the fact that her husband had died and left her nothing.

✿

During the First World War, Sophia saved her money; she kept the bills among the coffee beans and the chamomile flowers, she sewed them into the interlining of her plush coat, and she let them roam among the duck feathers of her four pillows. When Bobka was sixteen, he left school and took two jobs — one in the claque at the Opéra-Comique and the other as a helper in the projection room of a movie house. Having given his age (for the movie job) as nineteen, Bobka went around pasting and unpasting a thin mustache he had made up from the rat with which Sophia padded her long hair.

Delighted with his independent air and his modest but regular earnings, Sophia decided to leave him for a little while in Rosa's care and go check up on: 1) Zoltan, and 2) the financial status of Rosa's husband upon his death. The fact that there was a war on did not deter her for a moment.

She packed a small wicker trunk with four new costumes, pinned a rectangular pink satin envelope to the inside of her corset, folded into it a thick packet of bills, and set off in March of 1917, just as news of the overthrow of the Czarist government reached Paris.

Sophia took the Scandinavian route: through Denmark, Sweden, Finland, she made her way to Petrograd, and from there, through Moscow, Vilna, and Kiev, to Odessa. Like Hansel with his pebbles, she sowed the difficult path with her unimportant jewels. She left a little pearl brooch in the pocket of a ticket collector between Helsingfors and Petrograd, and in Kiev, in order to board a train already packed with troops, she unscrewed two small gold-and-turquoise pendants from her ears. She made the four-day trip between Paris and Odessa in three weeks.

＊

Standing in the lobby of the Lanzheron Hotel, on Richelieu Street, Sophia lifted Zoltan's last letter from the traveling bag she had taken out of Russia on her honeymoon seventeen years before, and checked Zoltan's room number. A few moments later, she knocked gently on his door; it was ajar and there was no answer, so she pushed it open. The first thing she did was to emit a long, low moan, like a dog's. Then she cried out. The cry receded to a raw whisper, and then became a moan again. And all the while she knocked her head sideways, rhythmically, against the doorframe. She tore off her hat. With her gloved hand she grasped a handful of her hair close to the roots, and tore that, too. At last she fell rigidly on her side in a dead faint.

＊

Zoltan took her to the Jewish Hospital, on Hospital Street, where she lay unconscious for almost a week. When she woke, her clenched and gloved fist slowly opened, and released a lock of reddish hair. But she could not move her legs. For another month she lay, almost motionless, almost unseeing, moaning and whispering, "No, no, I don't want to be introduced," when two heads kept appearing — Zoltan's, grown heavy in profile and curiously red (he had been standing at a window, looking out), and the young woman's as she turned, angular and posed obliquely, ready for flight (she had been pinning on her hat in front of an oval mirror).

And while Zoltan, between amateur choral rehearsals, stroked her stilled limbs and fed her sausages from a succession of shopping bags, Sophia, lying flat on her back, could not lose sight of that long, helpless pin, arrested in air. After six weeks in the hospital, Sophia got up and walked a little. She asked Zoltan to let her recuperate in his room at the Lanzheron Hotel. She studied the room carefully throughout her convalescence; she studied it from the depth of her despair, and yet with detachment, as one studies the family vault. She memorized the imagery on the wallpaper — branches of grapes intertwined with tarnished cherries, between lilacs in pale clusters and elongated baskets of fading pink roses.

She received Zoltan's family as well as her own, and they all treated her as if she were his widow, and herself risen from the dead. They brought her whatever provisions they could find — the town was now occupied by General Petlyura — and told her that Rosa's husband had died penniless. She received Madame Tauber, a childhood friend, who had once meant to be a pianist but had married an illustrious lawyer instead, and who came wearing her good pearls *under* her dress. Soon Sophia was well enough to move to a groundfloor apartment occupied by her widowed sister, Sema. It was a dangerous spot — near the station.

When the Bolsheviks removed Petlyura and declared a Soviet Republic, Sophia tacked a note on the door: "Here live two widows with three workers." One room of the apartment had been requisitioned and was in fact occupied by a worker. The two other workers were a student and an engineer, whom Sophia had decided to shelter and feed.

In March of 1918, the Germans came, the Hungarians and the Austrians came. Once more the town was occupied.

The Austrians, wearing white gloves, searched the apartment six times in all.

The two sisters managed to have enough food. Madame Tauber brought sausages and smoked fish; in the dining room sideboard Sophia hoarded stale loaves of bread. Madame Tauber managed to visit even after French, Polish, and Serbian troops were landed. The engineer Sophia was sheltering made friends with a French sailor, who gave him bits of frozen meat.

Madame Tauber laid her plans, and shared them with Sophia. In December of 1919, an Italian ship stood in the harbor ready to sail, and its captain, Madame Tauber's secret lover, offered to transport Sophia as well. When Zoltan came to say good-bye, she did not reproach him; she asked him to be kind, and send her a little money. Knowing that it would not be possible for him to do so, he promised. As it was raining, Sophia asked him to leave her his umbrella.

❋

At the Gare de Lyon, Bobka and Rosa stood waiting in the fog. Sophia stepped off the train, knelt on the pavement, and was about to kiss the ground when Bobka scurried forward; Rosa, deeply embarrassed, nudged Sophia's dirty coat with the tip of her pointed shoe.

A few days later, Sophia went shopping. She found a wallpaper that approximated her remembrance of grapes, tarnished cherries, and roses. In an open-air market, she bought a black lacquer Japanese box with an orange tassel, and on it, with a sharp nail instrument, she carved, in Russian: *"Pandona's* Secret." (She was incapable of retaining a foreign proper name exactly.) And in the box she placed the lock of her hair.

She had her bedroom repapered, she placed the box on

her bedside table, and next to it, within immediate reach, she propped Zoltan's umbrella. And so, inoculated against the past, she bandaged her legs and went to bed. She made Manitchka's wedding dress, and shed so many tears that it might have been a shroud she was hemming. Manitchka went on her honeymoon, secured forever to an affluent druggist, and soon after, Zinotchka left for Brussels, to fiddle for Professor Auer.

When Bobka started to sing in the chorus of the Opéra-Comique, he changed his name to Anatole Robert (Robert for Bobka, and Anatole for Anatole France). Sophia did not stir herself to hear him sing, either at the opera house or at one of his lessons, but Bobka, although hurt, was good to her. He handed over most of his earnings, and, without knowing accurately what ailed her, he often got down on one knee and promised her letters from Zoltan.

But when she was irascible and demanded to be waited on incessantly, when she moaned and loudly proclaimed herself a victim of Fate, he went off slamming doors. Neither he nor Rosa could distinguish between Sophia in a state of hysteria, truly paralyzed, and Sophia taking to her bed in search of culinary attentions and concentrated kindness. When the symptoms were genuine, she sewed a finer seam and slept better, but she suffered at all times. It was hard enough to have the power in her legs suddenly shut off by subliminal authorities over which she had no control (as if she had not paid the bill for so much water, gas, or electricity), but the worst of it was the certainty she had of having been chosen to pay not for her own but for Zoltan's sins.

❊

Bobka, tired of the two women, who so easily extinguished his merriment, married in great secrecy. He married a girl called Michoune, who had no hips and looked like a cozy young dog. She sang in a *boîte* with only one breast covered and did an imitation of Mistinguett singing "Il m'a vue nue . . . ta ra ram pa pa pa pam . . ." When he finally told Sophia, she took it so calmly that it seemed she had heard it all before. She tapped Bobka gently on the wrist and begged him not to give Michoune all of his earnings; then she held his wrist lightly in her hand and reminded him not to forget her — reminded him that she was his mother, and had sacrificed herself for him.

Rosa marked the occasion by moving to a small apartment five houses away, taking with her a great deal of furniture, and in the moving a gilded mirror was shattered. Sophia wept, superstitiously, and over her impending solitude.

*

From then on, during the winter Sophia hibernated. In the morning, she slowly propped herself up against her four pillows, and sewed detailed bed linen when she was well, in order to receive in style when she was not. She also made herself three summer dresses. Rosa came. (She did all the marketing.) Bobka came. (Sophia refused to meet Michoune.) The postman came at rare intervals, and, because Sophia lived alone, was greeted with tremulous effusions.

Very seldom, she went out to dinner, at the Marshaks', and embarrassed them, because she was no longer used to social amenities, by interrupting Professor Marshak's Egyptian recollections with shouts of impossible laughter.

Every summer she packed her trunk and went off to take the waters. Often she persuaded Rosa, who suffered from ordinary aches and pains, to come along. The cures were Sophia's great luxury. Over the years, she went to Baden, she went to Carlsbad, she went to Baden-Baden. In 1927,

Sophia and Rosa were photographed standing in white sunshine against gray grass in Wiesbaden — Sophia in a light crêpe dress that circled her ankles unevenly. Around her neck she wore a modest chain that plunged right down to her knee and there terminated in a lorgnette. Under the wide Panama hat her face was ferociously sad, almost heroic. Her hand gripped the pommel of Zoltan's half-open umbrella.

❀

On the night of April first, in the year 1930, Michoune, having sung her imitation of Mistinguett singing "Il m'a vue nue . . . ta ra ram pa pa pa pam . . ." pointed toward the wings and introduced Anatole Robert. Bobka had a sinister way of walking onstage; he moved sideways, like a sneak, as if half of him had to be dragged in by the other half.

Small like Sophia, hed-haired like Zoltan, and dressed in tight-fitting tails, he stood silent in front of the microphone. A muffled drum rolled, the pianist started to complain in a minor key, and at the moment when the audience was primed for Bobka's first note, there came instead an insulting whispered syllable: "Pnoo." The drum stood deserted, the pianist's left hand fell into his lap. "Chee-ta-mi," Bobka continued. "Kal-pa-kanoo." The audience was silent. Then, as if he were teaching the deaf and dumb, accenting every syllable with his right hand, the index and middle fingers against his thumb, Bobka repeated, "Pnoo, chee-ta-mi, kal-pak, a-noo." He played the part of a man who has stumbled into some unknown climate where speech is mechanical, important, and meaningless. "Pnoochee, tamikal, pakanoo," he said suddenly, changing the beat, and now he played the part of a driver at the wheel of a machine, obliged to open a path through the audience. "Pnoo, chee-ta-mi, kal-pak, a-noo," Bobka said, fast. Faster and faster, until his body was burning and his face had reached that shade of apoplectic red it had worn in childhood when he ran all the way from Vera Marshak's to the Rue de La Fayette. "Pnoocheetamikalpakanoo!" he finally cried out, with the power and the speed of a dark train running at midnight through an abandoned station. But he was not alone, and the train was halted with an agony of brakes as the applause smashed into the ears of Anatole Robert, and he let all the syllables run into one another. "Bravo! Bis! Bis!" they shouted.

Bobka had arrived. He made a fortune. He wore a ring with a star sapphire, acquired a miniature borzoi, and wound Michoune in silver fox.

*

Sophia became a personage; she stayed in bed and sewed for pleasure. The lady members of The Fellows of Odessa came to visit, and she started a collection of porcelain boxes, so that they would know what to bring. They also brought sausages, Greek olives without too much salt, and books from the Russian library.

Bobka took care of all her needs, and at last she could write exultant letters to Zoltan. She entertained the postman with her son's successes, and even offered him a quick glass of dark tea sweetened with a teaspoon of raspberry jam. But one morning he brought a terrible letter from Bobka, who was touring the provinces. Michoune had gambled in Monte Carlo, and in three nights had lost all his money. Bobka returned to Paris without her, changed his syllables, and, in time, made another fortune. Sophia grew fat and voluble, and persuaded Bobka to take back Michoune. Rosa came to cook enormous meals, and Zinotchka, flitting through Paris on her way to London, came with her fiddle, and played "The Flight of the Bumblebee."

Bobka went touring again and did not write; for several months no one knew where he was, until the postman brought another terrible letter, penned by Michoune in Bordeaux. Anatole Robert had abandoned her. But this time it was he who had gambled away their money. The tour had been a flop, the impresario had walked out on them in Toulon. "Anatole" had pulled himself together, dropped his syllables, and tried all the rulers of all the Russias, but in vain; no one was interested in the act. In despair, unable to pay his debts, he had borrowed money for his passage and fled to New York, where he had a friend in real estate. He had left a note for her, telling her to get in touch with his mother, who would help her. The next time the postman came with a letter from Zoltan, Sophia entrusted him with a packet of bank notes to be sent to Michoune in his name.

Sophia complained only to Rosa, but the Marshaks soon heard, and informed the lady members of The Fellows of Odessa, who came less often.

*

Although Sophia seemed to manage perfectly well without Rosa, when an occasional visitor came to sit at her bedside she complained endlessly — of her attacks of paralysis, of rheumatic pains in her back, arthritis in her fingers, and green circles in front of her eyes.

After describing her symptoms in great detail, she would shift the monologue, first to Bobka and then to Zoltan, to the acute boredom of the listener, who invariably thought them better forgotten. She kept Bobka's letters under her pillows. He had, upon his arrival in New York, been recommended, by his friend in real estate, to the owner of the Troika, on

Thirteenth Street, A. F. Kamarovsky, who had given him a job as a waiter. But he did not remain a waiter long. No, he was soon doing the syllables act twice an evening. A friend of Gregory Ratoff had caught the act, and now Bobka was about to be given a screen test for the short singing part of a carpet seller, and perhaps even for the longer, straight part of a tailor, in a new movie based on *The Arabian Nights.* Sophia never forgot to mention that whenever Bobka wrote he included a money order.

She kept Zoltan's letters in the Japanese lacquer box, and she read passages from them aloud to visitors, without the slightest provocation.

The Bolsheviks were back, and there was a famine. Though Zoltan loved to flee, when everyone tried to escape in the January 1920 "evacuation," he stayed. He was now singing in the chorus of the Odessa Opera, there was no heat, and singers and spectators wore their coats. The unrest and confusion of the town, Zoltan wrote, had penetrated into the Opera House. They were singing Rubinstein's *Demon* in the evening and *Eugen Onegin* in the afternoon. It was the last act — the duet between Gremin and Onegin. Gremin had begun his aria and, in the tradition of Russian bassos, was gently tapping out the rhythm with his foot. The technical crew below, forgetting which opera was being done, mistook the tapping for a cue, and Onegin slowly sank into the dark regions that were reserved for *Demon.* Sophia never tired of reading that anecdote. She always laughed hard, for a very long time, and when she had no strength left, she would start rocking to the sound *tststststs,* hardly audible, but the sound would carry her, for another stretch of time, to the ebb of merriment.

Zoltan had become an elusive, beloved friend of her childhood who had gone beyond the boundaries of her own life, and she spoke of him with infinite nostalgia. She still counted her money carefully, and took to sewing it into the draperies.

❋

But when the cold sky of her last winter broke and a gentle rain fell day after day, with its promise of a lily-of-the-valley smell for May, something unexpected happened: Sophia softly woke from her past sufferings and fell in love with the postman. He was not irresponsible. If there was a letter or a money order, or both, he came. It was as simple as that.

She began to rouge the fine skin of her cheeks — which had never known disguise before — with bright pink powder. When she had to be fitted for an upper set of false teeth, six weeks before her death, Sophia assured the woman dentist (a friend of the Marshaks') that the only laws in nature were unevenness and unexpectedness. Her new teeth were constructed accordingly — shorter on one side than on the other.

Every morning at the appointed hour, she crossed a pink dressing gown far over her large bosom, and, leaning on Zoltan's umbrella, waited for the postman at the window. Time had healed her broken heart to the point where she could now express a sentiment toward a man, and the postman was the only man she saw. When he did not come, as on most mornings, she was not disappointed. The lady members of The Fellows of Odessa were slightly jolted by Sophia's unseasonable coquetry, but she seemed, to them, at last in peace.

Toward the end of April, Sophia had a heart attack. The landlady called Rosa, who was now seventy-five and took forty minutes to climb the six flights. She spent three nights in an armchair by Sophia's bed, because she did not trust herself to go up the stairs again. When she was certain that Sophia would recover, she sat down at the table by the window and wrote to Zoltan and to Bobka, telling them what had happened, and asking them to write only of light and happy events, and not to worry Sophia under any circumstances.

On her last morning, Sophia said aloud, "Today I shall have a letter from Zoltan." She spat another sunflower seed: "Tfoo!" And she began to sing again: "Dai, dai, de-rai, dai, dai . . ." She stopped to listen. Her door was ajar, and she heard footsteps climbing — almost running — up the stairs, and they were unfamiliar. She had not heard from Bobka for some time, but an unsummoned image, that of Zoltan, avid and strange, running up those same stairs, immediately came to her mind. Sophia held her sewing in midair. The footsteps on the stairs were not the postman's. But whose were they, then?

"Come in, come in!" said Sophia, consciously using the voice she used for the postman. By the uniform she recognized a telegraph boy, new, young, who had not witnessed the rainbow of her life, and had resentfully climbed six flights to find, at the end, a frightened old woman in bed. "Thank you, thank you . . ." said Sophia, conscious of her accent. She held the telegram in her right hand, and she waved it slightly in an attempt to dismiss him. The telegraph boy did not leave. Sophia looked under her pillow, found two francs, handed them to him, and in her confusion said, "For tea," in Russian, instead of the French "For a drink." With a sense of terror, she realized that she had, in this moment of contact with an unknown young telegraph boy, lost her sense of time.

He started slowly down the stairs, and Sophia was alone, holding in her hand a little rectangle of blue paper. Hesitantly she placed it on her night table. She unscrewed the top of her medicine bottle, and into her full water glass she squeezed approximately twenty-five valerian drops. (Their sad, caustic smell always held for her a promise of quietude.) The drops swam to the bottom of the glass, and Sophia waited until they had risen to the surface in a thin brown cloud, but she could not wait any longer to open the telegram. She read the message twice; under stress she never registered a statement the first time. "Your Bobby very sick pneumonia but now out of danger." It was signed "Kamarovsky."

Sophia leaned forward, then she leaned back; she moaned, rocking back and forth for a moment, almost chanting her grief and joy. When she felt herself falling forward, she reached for the valerian drops, but her arm fell short. The baskets of roses on the wallpaper, the grapes and cherries, moved and merged. She fell in a whirl, yet something was obstructing the total dizziness of her fall — some huge being in pain, floating, then floundering, inside her chest, unable to escape, yet barring her own way. Sophia would not let it. She tore at it with her hand, and soon she knew that she had throttled it, and that she could now fall back into the serenity of her four pillows. She had been dead only a few seconds when the telegraph boy reached the bottom of the stairs and walked out into the street and met the postman, who stood very still on the pavement, looking for a letter in his box; as the telegraph boy went past, the postman looked up at him, brought Zoltan's letter to his kepi, and saluted — a small gesture of contempt.

By a Lake in the Bois

T HE GIRL WAS ELEVEN and ineffably lovely, with straight
flaxen hair, freckles, and very sad blue eyes. Her hair
was parted in the middle from her forehead to the nape of
her neck, and held by two rubber bands. She sat at the edge
of her wrought-iron chair as if she waited for something important to happen; there was a taut quality to her body, an
ardent look about her mouth and her nostrils. She was
dressed like a very much younger child, in a short pleated
skirt and Lacoste shirt and sandals. (But then, most of the
sixteen-year-olds, and the twenty-year-olds, were suddenly
dressed just like her.) What went on underneath the shirt
was her secret. Each time she dressed and undressed, and
at other times too, she knew that the nipples of her breasts
were full. This had just happened; hardly a week had passed
since she had noticed, and she had not told a soul.

The boy was nine. He blinked a lot in the sunlight. His
eyelashes were pale and extremely long and had no curl
to them. They did not look like human eyelashes, but they
were beautiful, like the eyelashes on a llama or a kangaroo.

They fell incessantly, fan shaped, hiding the blue skin under his eyes. He would learn, in time, to use them, until he would have to learn to forget them. But he didn't know about them yet. So they were not his secret. In the meantime the boy couldn't keep still. "I'm so thirsty," he said.

For no apparent reason, as if moving to a sleepwalker's dream, his mother started to get up from her chair, and his father immediately took her by the wrist and made her sit down again.

The boy watched them. He got up very early in the morning, and lately, just lately, he had heard a muffled sound coming from his parents' room. Once, after his father, looking tired in the morning, had left for the office, he had simply walked into his parents' bedroom, left his plush monkey on his mother's night table, and walked out again.

So, his mother cried in bed, early in the morning. Why in the morning? Wasn't it better to cry at night, when everything was dark? In any case, he had not told his sister, who more than slept: she hibernated like a badger and never was anxious to get up. He had not told anybody, so that was one of his secrets, but not the only one. He had many.

They had been in Paris for two days.

"I'm thirsty," the boy repeated.

A waiter, with sweat on his upper lip, stood by their table.

"English?" asked the boy's father, who was English. His heavy eyebrows rose. He could speak French, but at times he did not feel like it.

"But of course," said the waiter.

"All right," said the man. He looked at his wife, and at the two children. Without asking anyone anything, he said, "One orangeade, two lemonades, one beer, please." Then he took off his blazer, unknotted his tie, and opened the top button of his shirt.

The lake in the Bois was the cold green of legendary lakes. But the sky was contemporary, clear, joyous, and blue, with a few white clouds moving lightly from right to left.

The woman looked up. "It's hot," she said. Then, after a moment's silence, she added, to no one in particular, "The skies in France do seem to lie lower than anywhere else."

Her daughter moved forward, to the very edge of her chair, and eagerly asked, "Do you think *that's* why the Gauls always thought the sky was going to fall on their heads?" Then she sat back in her chair and giggled.

"Nothing to do with it," the boy answered, fidgeting.

The woman said nothing. Her world had shrunk. Its proportions were all wrong, and it had nothing to do with the fact that the Paris sky, as opposed to the London sky, seemed to hover too close to the top of her head. Only she knew the exact proportions of the change, but the change itself was no secret to her family. She looked around her — at the lake and at a weeping willow, and at her husband — and tried to forget.

The rowboats were all painted white and they all moved in the same direction, from right to left.

"Why do you think all the rowboats are moving from right to left?" the woman asked.

"How would I know?" her husband answered, without a trace of malice.

The young boys who rowed wore long tight trousers and their chests were bare. Most of them were alone. A few had a girl with them — a girl with very long hair and bangs and an invisible face. The man sat and watched the rowers carefully, and pronounced them all quite fit, a happy change from the way French youth looked before the last war.

The little boy pointed to his wrist and said, "That's my very finest mosquito bite."

"That's ridiculous," his sister said. Then she added, "You're *all* bitten."

The waiter distributed bottles and glasses, getting them slightly mixed up, except for the beer. He said, "One beer, two lemonades, one orangeade." After he left, one lemonade bottle was silently exchanged for the bottle of orangeade.

The man wiped his horn-rimmed, slightly smoked glasses, held the wings of his nose between his thumb and his forefinger for a moment, and put the glasses in a pocket of the blazer, which hung, neatly, on the back of his wrought-iron chair. Then, from another pocket, he brought out matches and a pack of cigarettes.

"You're smoking too much," the woman said.

The man inhaled, deeply. "I know," he said, without a trace of irritation.

"We all look so tired," the woman said, and smiled.

"We've only just arrived," the man said. After a while he added, "Besides, everybody looks tired."

Everyone did. It was the end of July. A pale and muscular young man, wearing a pair of red bikini bathing trunks and nothing else, came off the boat that had crossed the lake from the opposite bank.

Suddenly, the boy shouted, "Oh look! Ducks! *Ducks!*" Five ducks had wandered up from the water and moved about confidently from table to table, waiting to be fed. "I'm going to feed the ducks," said the boy.

It was hot now, and the restaurant was almost full. The girls' skirts were as short as their hair was long. They wore no lipstick. The boys' hair was shaggy and dirty. The girls looked languorous. They never spoke. At times they slowly moved their heads back, and then the boys moved toward them and very slowly kissed them.

The woman felt strangely old and out of place. Her hair

was wrong and her skirt longer than it should have been. Mere details, but she was conscious of them.

She watched an older couple, who sat across from one another and spoke to each other, together and at the same time. The man wore no shirt; he had a tremendous and flabby pink chest, and he drank his beer out of the bottle. His wife's eyebrows were drawn on with a pencil, and for some reason she drank mineral water out of a cup.

"Daddy, Mummy, look at the models!" said the little girl, pointing with her empty lemonade glass.

None of them had seen the crew disembark, or settle down, or start to work. Perhaps they had walked over from another part of the island. Now two models walked by the very edge of the lake, skirts mid thigh, topped by turtleneck sweaters, and, lastly, hats. They were modeling next autumn's or next winter's hats.

The little girl stood up and giggled. The giggle soon turned into a laugh. She put her hand in front of her mouth.

"Sit down," said her mother.

She sat down, and in a moment was serious.

Next autumn or next winter. The woman did not know where she, where they, would be next autumn or next winter. She lived each hour by the minute. At times, in the past two days, she had found it an effort to draw the next breath. That could be counted in seconds. Ridiculous. She twisted her diamond ring once around her finger. It felt tight. She twisted her wedding ring. She looked at the models. She looked at their hats.

The photographer, with a limp and a stoop, moved back from the models as they came toward him. He was small and incredibly frail, with a tight grayish face and a narrow circle of hair that looked like a tonsure. He was shooting with a movie camera.

"Oh, Mummy, those hats!" said the girl.

One model, who had a rabbity mouth and smoked a cigarette as she walked, wore an emerald green bowler with a rim lined in cheetah. The bowler had long earflaps of cheetah that narrowed down until they buttoned under the chin. The other model wore a bowler too — a royal purple one, of plushy felt, without earflaps. Both models had fresh sun tans.

The little girl stood up again to look. The man put out his cigarette and looked at his wife. After the models', her skin looked extraordinarily pale. He put his arm around her shoulder and said, "Don't look so desperate."

"But I'm not," she answered stupidly, trying not to be.

The man looked at her. She had grown wider somehow, in the past few years, without getting at all plump. Perhaps those strange miscarriages had done it. How distasteful. And those laugh lines, deeply etched suddenly, at the corners of her mouth — a sign of crisis; she was too young for that. As he watched her, the man's feelings alternated between concern and a curious neutrality that bordered on distaste. For the truth was, he loved another, who was straight, simple, narrow, and tall. That was his secret. His wife couldn't possibly know. What she did know was silence, their present silent enmity. But she was reacting badly. Very badly. This sudden helplessness; those morning tears. He watched the rowboats. He thought of his sailboat in drydock, and wished he were on it, somewhere on the Mediterranean, anywhere, but alone, at sea.

Two swans appeared, swimming slowly from right to left.

"Fab, those ducks. I want one," said the boy, looking at the swans.

For a while, nobody spoke.

Then the boy began twisting on his chair.

"Sit still," said his mother.

He did. He faced both his parents squarely and then he asked, "If you two die, where do I go?"

His mother laughed. She said, "What a stupid question!"

His father said, very directly, "Why stupid? After all, the child has a right to know."

The girl sat back in her chair until her spine made a lovely curve, and then she smiled a demonic smile, which her mother, who happened to be watching, failed to understand. Children were so often incomprehensible. Incomprehensible brought her to sensible. That's what she had — a sensible, English attitude toward children. After all, given the proper amount of time, they would grow up.

The man was speaking. "All right," he said. "You go to your godparents." At that point, the woman caught up with what he was saying.

"Who are my godparents?" asked the boy, as if he didn't know.

"The Wilders," said his mother.

"You haven't seen them, because they've been to the States — for a year and a half. But they should be back by November," said his father.

"She's fat," said the boy. And as an afterthought, to his mother, "And I heard you tell Daddy she was pretty lazy."

The girl giggled. Then she began to bite her thumbnail.

"Stop that," said her father.

"And Mr. Wilder has a disease," the boy said. "I don't want to live with an obese person and a man with a disease."

There was a momentary silence. Then the father said, "Go and explore something, both of you." They went off. Then to his wife, who seemed to be holding back new tears, the man, who was beginning to feel quite detached, said, "Please, dear, make an effort, if only for the children."

She did. She, who felt she had always loved so well, suddenly couldn't love. For the large, graying, green-eyed man at her side, whom she had loved forever it seemed, she didn't know what she felt. A few weeks ago, she had known; soon again she would know. But at this very moment, she did not. Eternity had sprung a corner, and that was a secret nobody knew.

"Guess how long it took me to get over there and explore?" asked the boy, pointing to the weeping willow. "Forty-five seconds," he said, answering his own question.

The girl primly smoothed the pleats of her skirt against her behind as she sat down at the very edge of her chair.

"You didn't take much of a walk," said their father.

The model with the rabbity mouth sat down alone at one of the coffee tables against a hedge and took long looks at herself in a rectangular mirror. A stylist, wearing a flowing flowered muumuu and cork-soled wedgies, opened an enormous carton named Georgette and took out a Garbo hat, which she carefully put on the model. It was beige felt, with a giant, black velvet question mark that began at the crown and then flowed on and on until it stopped, only to be followed by a period placed at the very edge of the brim.

The photographer gave directions. The model placed her elbows on the table and her knuckles under her chin. She bent her head down, and then her face disappeared completely and only the hat was visible, the giant question mark against the neutral felt. The photographer grew very voluble and very excited. Then he began to shoot, still using a movie camera.

The little girl asked, "What is the percentage on orphans?"

"I'm sick of this conversation," said her father.

Four Swedes disembarked, all perfectly blond and tall;

one pink skinned and dressed in army fatigues but all four of them unmistakable Swedes. They found a table and immediately began a conversation in Swedish.

The girl said, "Where are the ducks? I don't see them."

"Let's go look!" said the boy.

"No, we're going back to the hotel," said their father.

The woman looked up at the sky. The clouds, still moving from right to left, were growing darker. Darker clouds, tinged with pink, and then the woman knew, by the edge of a lake in the Bois, by the edge of an abyss, that neither today nor tomorrow, but someday, soon perhaps, it would happen, and that she did not have the power to keep it from happening. It was going to happen, and then the children would, in a way, be half-orphaned. So there it was, no longer a secret, and now that she knew, it would no longer be necessary to cry.

"Collect everything," the man said. Then he too looked up at the sky. "The wind is changing," he said.

Acacias

I LOVE TO READ cookbooks. I am addicted to them, in the way other people are addicted to detective stories. I love the rapidly unfolding plots, I rarely quarrel with the style, and the very nature of the vocabulary enchants me. I read, toward the end of a recipe for "Sylphides de volaille," ". . . push the sylphs into the oven, keep them there four to five minutes . . ."

I attend the death and apotheosis of an eggplant. What violence: "Peel, cut into rather thin slices, sprinkle with salt, let drain for several hours, then drench in flour and fry in boiling oil."

An unfolding recipe is, to the mind's eye, a miraculous thing to watch; "Take a half a pound of flour . . ." I take it, I sprinkle it on a white formica counter top; I have a shape, a hill, white on white — chalk, plaster, powder fit for the face of a clown; perhaps a child will make a flour-and-salt map of the continent of Australia, but no. In thirty-one seconds I have read on to the dénouement, and what do I have? A Norman apple tart.

I love the oblique cookbooks — the ones that keep deviating all the time. One of my favorites is called *L'Art Culinaire Français par Nos Grands Maîtres de la Cuisine.* A thread of mystery runs through that book as I follow an enigmatic progression of cakes all named Progrès — Fonds de Progrès (Ga.) (*pour huit personnes*), page 682; Progrès (D. & D.) (*pour quinze personnes*), page 716; Progrès (P.) page 719; Progrès chocolat (J.), page 742; Progrès praliné (J.), page 743. They are not consecutive and the only clue to the mystery is the common use of crushed almonds. I observe more cakes, which appear to obey the moods of love — Jalousies, page 735; Puits d'amour, page 743; Soupirs, page 744.

Toward the end of the book I find the heading "Cuisine Etrangère." Under "America," a canned-pineapple salad, and under "Russia" in the section on Jewish cooking, a recipe for "Halé," a holiday, or holy day bread. It is a frightfully long and very devious recipe. *Halé* is at first compared to everyday black bread. Then memory is brought in (still no ingredients), then childhood, then the feel of hot potatoes in the pockets of winter coats, and finally, anticipating the emergence of the *halé* from the oven, this heavy-handed, compressed, but quasi-Proustian sentence: ". . . perhaps he will imagine the odors of the hours of his youth, both good and bad, but as sweetly remembered as the perfume of blooming acacias in Odessa."

Involuntarily, I shut my eyes and close the book. The next sentence would have read, "Let us return to our *halé*." But no, let us not return to our *halé*. Let us turn, instead, to my grandmother.

She sat very straight in her chair, with a pillow behind her back, and slowly, very slowly, her right hand, which held a neatly folded handkerchief with which she wiped her forehead when she came out of the kitchen — her right hand came up, index finger pointed toward her temple, until it stopped at the exact gesture with which a child pretends to shoot itself. She held it there a moment, and then, invariably, she said, "Ah, those acacias, those acacias. Ah, the scent of those acacia trees."

The index-finger-to-the-temple gesture represented wonder, astonishment, disbelief, and bewildering beauty. The voice was lyrical, slightly more breathy than usual. After the acacias, after the long silence that followed them, she always said, "Think of that." And the hand, still holding the neat square of handkerchief, fell very quietly to her lap, palm up. Then came another long silence, until at last her eyes narrowed and became veiled. That, like a movie dissolve, was the signal for flashback.

The recurring theme of the acacia trees stood for memory. From the acacia trees she always moved back, but I could never tell where she was going. Patiently, I had to wait until she took me there. Together we roamed the shores of the Black Sea, walked the docks in Odessa, lived through a pogrom and a famine, spent our summers at a dacha, emigrated to Constantinople and there went for a swim, and so on, until we had come full circle and were back on the shores of the Black Sea.

I visualized her reminiscences as fully acted plays, with costumes and sets. I was particularly fond of the move from Odessa to the dacha. This play was called *Three Furnished Months by the Black Sea,* and the opening scene showed a mountain of beds, chests, desks, bundles of clothes, silver, a samovar (although she never mentioned it), china, pots and pans, neat layers of Persian shawls, all piled onto an open van. The maid sat balanced on top, holding an indefinite bird in a cage, looking down over the edge of this precipice, and singing. They could barely move, the horse was so old. This allowed me plenty of time to observe the landscape. It was flat and arid, half Turkish and half Greek (although it certainly shouldn't have been), with a few ruins, a few stunted trees. High above the van, the sun shone, and there was not one cloud.

❋

Of course, I did not know my grandmother — Boubinka — in her youth. Perhaps, as a small child living in France, I had seen and smelled acacia trees. But I did not remember them. At the time of the reminiscences, when I was eleven or twelve, all I knew about acacias was that they had the magic power to precipitate, both violently and sweetly, old people back to their youth. But that was not enough. So I invented an acacia. It was a tall tree with a trunk like a birch's, but dappled light brown and white. Its branches were delicately drawn. It was a serene tree, with a tremendous amount of blossoms; the flowers were not unlike apple blossoms, but quite large and very white. The scent of my acacia was white, too — white and heavy, a mixture of jasmine and tuberose, with jasmine predominating, and in order to counterbalance the sweetness of tuberose, I added a little grated rind, from both the lemon and the lime.

About a year ago, I opened the *Encyclopædia Britannica* and looked up the acacia. I learned that it is a genus of trees and shrubs belonging to the pea family; that the leaves are bipinnate; that the seeded, podlike fruits are either flattened or cylindrical; and that the flowers are small, arranged in rounded or elongated clusters, and frequently fragrant. (Frequently! Why, one branch of any one of my acacia trees would have sufficed to perfume my present apartment. Nor was I too fond of the idea that the acacia can be a shrub.) The *Encyclopædia* made but a very small dent in my imagination. Someday soon, I know, I shall see an acacia tree. Immediately, and yet slowly, the new image, the new scent, will obliterate the old. But in the meantime, let me keep my tree.

❋

I shared a small apartment with my grandmother; she slept in the living room, on a couch. And it was in that room that she sat in her chair by the dining table, with the pillow behind her back, and I sat curled up in a chair by the window, biting my nails. Homework was done, and it was time for supper. I could smell eggplant salad. First the smell of eggplant cooking, then the smell of vinaigrette poured onto the chopped eggplants while they were still hot. But the table, although laid, was empty. No eggplant, no Russian meatballs. She sat watching me; and then, directly, without mentioning the acacias, she said, "After that, I married the wrong man, a man I did not love, and that is a terrible sin, and I paid for it the rest of my life."

It was the epilogue to an earlier, tragic, and long episode she had told me about a few days before, and that was why she had not mentioned the acacias.

❋

The set changes and it is dark. I am torn between Boubinka's story and Turgenev's "First Love." Actually, they are not dissimilar. But my grandmother's story is called *First and Only Love Betrayed*. The set is dark but for one window on the first floor of an otherwise black house. In that window, under a yellow, almost ochre light, I see a man and a woman kiss. Then the man pulls away. He has dead black hair, a dense black mustache, an exceedingly white skin, so white and mat it looks heavily powdered, but not with flour like a baker boy's; quite the contrary, this young man has deep-yellow eyes and the sylphlike elegance of a young necromancer. I see the woman from the back; she wears a yellow dress that matches his eyes and the light under which they have just kissed. The man is the only man my grandmother ever loved, and the woman is the one with whom he betrays her. (She has no further identity.) And silhouetted vaguely against the dark house, stage left, stands Boubinka, aged eighteen. She stands alone, in a pale orchid ball dress, leaning on a folded black umbrella. (No, no symbolism, please; it is too easy, far too easy, and probably meaningless.) She has seen it all, seen them kiss under that yellow light that did not warm them. She screams and faints. No, she doesn't. She swoons; she crumples up into the folds of that orchid dress as softly as egg whites folding into batter. But then, a split second later, I hear the dry snap of the umbrella handle as it hits the pavement. And for a while after that nothing happens, because the story really stopped where Boubinka said, "I saw them — I saw them, and that was the end."

So there she is, on the ground. Later, she regains consciousness. She gets up slowly, does not brush the dirt off her orchid ball dress; nor does she straighten her hat, because I do not make her wear one. Leaning on her folded umbrella, painfully, somehow, she makes her way home.

"I was terribly sick for weeks after that."

I see her in bed with a high fever, and she doesn't care whether she lives or dies. Her nightdress is rumpled, her bed linen is not embroidered. The family is large, and there is only one servant girl in the kitchen. Boubinka lies in bed, wasting. The bloom and the dew are both gone from her orchid cheeks. The doctor says she is dying of love, and there is nothing he can do. A succession of faceless sisters, cousins, and aunts brings her a succession of broths, which she leaves untouched.

Then one day, one bright day — it must have been in the spring — she feels hungry and gets up. Perhaps she spied, in the warmer air, a hint of beloved acacias? When, exactly, do they bloom? No matter. Spring was her least favorite season; it made her tearful and short-tempered. Perhaps it had seen the death of her young dream (I'm almost certain that it did) and her return to a different life, in a world that appeared suddenly harsh to her, and rigid, and against which, from that moment on, she felt she must continually fight. She gets up and goes to the kitchen. Then she tells an older suitor that she will marry him, and she does. He has a well-cared-for, pointed beard, and she marries him in her orchid dress, but her cheeks no longer match it, and she cries.

Why couldn't I give her the beautifully sad and white wedding dress that she deserved? I sewed complicated clothes for my dolls, but my grandmother in her youth, summer and winter, morning, noon, and evening, had to wear her orchid ball dress, until one day I looked at her and realized that she was quite old and wore black, usually printed with an almost microscopic print of indecipherable flowers.

❁

Before she became old, she was ageless for a long time, especially at night. She sat through the white nights of my childhood, and told me stories. Cold, weary, heavy-featured, and uncomplaining, the wart on the side of her nose more visible than it was during the day, she sat by my bed, with her dressing gown over her shoulders, and told me stories. They were marvelous stories, and I can't remember a single one. The only thing I do remember is that they were her own. They had nothing to do with fairy tales. No goldfish ever spoke from the end of a fishing line, no princess with corn-silk hair moaned over her fate in a dungeon, and certainly no one slept for a hundred years. Forced into sleeplessness, she was unwilling to let others rest.

And so am I. I do not feel that what is called final rest is particularly inviolate, and so I still summon her, at times, in the middle of the night when I have time to think. She has been dead two years now.

Often at night I said, "Don't tell me a story. Let us talk."

"All right. Let us talk."

By then she was old, and had a tendency to be repetitious.

"He betrayed me; the man I loved betrayed me."

"Yes, I know."

"Did you know that I was eighteen at the time, and considered myself an old maid?"

"Yes, I know."

"So that I had to marry right away?"

"Yes."

"And I was miserable."

＊

A wide avenue in Odessa makes up the set of the acacia trees. The play is called *Family Life*. The trees are once more in bloom and the perspective is wide open. The houses have only one or two floors. The set is conservative — hackneyed, even. It looks as if it had been begun by Utrillo and finished by Vertès. It isn't a very good set, I admit, but there she is, I see her — Boubinka! — with three gloved children holding on to her orchid skirts, and the youngest, my mother — for it must be (think of that!) — in a pram with big wheels. Boubinka stops to speak to a friend. They both have wide, beautiful bosoms. The friend has one child, with a runny nose. Boubinka's children all look healthy. They all have her gray-blue eyes flecked with yellow near the iris, and bright lavender cheeks. But at home, everything changes. The set, an interior, is in dark brown and gloomy plush. The husband prays and wears a black skullcap. Boubinka wants to laugh (she is only twenty-five; she must laugh; she will explode if she doesn't), but *no one* laughs. The children are hushed when they cry. It disturbs their father at his prayers. His face is in darkness; only his mouth moves. The children walk on tiptoe, with furtive eyes.

And what inspired *Family Life?* Where did I gather the broken blossoms of her life? They must have fallen silently onto the stage from the trees of the acacia set. Strange, because she actually said very little about that period of her life.

*

I owned and lost a small photograph, only slightly faded in color — a miniature, really — of Boubinka at fifteen. (Where, oh, where does such a prodigious object disappear? I wanted it reframed; we moved, and I never saw it again.) Her hair was cropped short after an attack of typhus; it was curly and bright yellow-gold in color. The eyes were gray-blue and slanted, the nose very short and flat, with a round tip, the mouth narrow, prim, adult, with lines at the corners. And here at last I must grant her a change of dress. She wore nattier blue, with a collar so high it almost reached her ears, and long rows of small buttons aligned down the front.

I have lost the miniature, but in my loose-leaf cookbook I find the following recipe:

Boubinka's Eggplant

Place two medium-sized eggplants into warm water to cover. Cook until soft. Drain carefully. Place eggplants between two breadboards. Place dictionary on top of that. Let cool. Wait awhile. Take meat out with a spoon. Chop it carefully, thoroughly. Salt. Pepper. Grated onion. Transfer to bowl or whatever. Add Wesson oil and Premier wine vinegar.

＊

The acacia trees never appeared while she had work to do. She had isolated her youth, carefully wrapped it in their scent, and transplanted it, first to Paris and then to New York. But memory only answers to reflection, to pause. She had to sit down in her chair, and, after a certain silence, raise her finger to her temple, and begin. But she did not always have the necessary time.

She shopped. She shopped every day. Sometimes she went to market in order to buy two bunches of carrots she had been told would be on sale that day. There were several small grocers, close to one another, on Madison Avenue in the upper Nineties. She would temporarily abandon one for the other, and that one for a third, sometimes edging closer to home, sometimes moving farther away. "Thieves," she muttered regularly in Russian, "all a bunch of thieves." She had a large black change purse, and she carried a great deal of money in coins, because she always tried to pay the exact sum. "Wait," she said, and looked until she found a penny in one of her pockets.

She dressed well to go to market. She had a decent fur for the winter, and for the summer a navy blue, silk coat that I loved, and a succession of dark hats, navy blue or black, straw or felt, depending on the season, and decorated, as they were in those days, with a poor replica of a bird, or a small bouquet of patent-leather flowers, which, being a neat sewer, I was allowed to sew on myself. She looked tired at the grocer's — small, quite elegant; and I was proud when she turned and turned an orange in her hand, because so few of them lived up to her idea of perfection, and in silence, deep down in me as I watched her, I knew that I did.

She bought a lot of potatoes, not too many vegetables — eggplants, cucumbers, a few zucchinis in season. She bought fruit, and she bought fresh meat every shopping day. Butchers gave her more trouble even than grocers. She found meat prices exorbitant in New York, and she was capable of buying a slice of calf's liver for herself at one butcher's and a slice for me at another's, to compare both the price and quality of the meat, and then she could call one butcher an even bigger thief than the other.

She did a lot of frying in butter mixed with a bit of salad oil. She only bought familiar cuts of meat. She made a good pot roast, but she mistrusted the oven, and the broiler she never bothered about, so she really only cooked on top of the stove. A chicken was boiled or stewed, and chopped meat was fried into Russian meatballs, which she gave me day in and day out, and which I never tired of. She seldom made desserts, and I did not crave them. She gave me now and then a piece of chocolate, or, on rare occasions, made a batch of apple fritters. She would not give me the recipe for this. "Too complicated," she said.

She made scallop of veal, and calf's liver in the pan, which is the best way of making liver, but she never knew that a vegetable, or rice, or a potato, should accompany the meat. She made a potato salad for an hors d'oeuvre, or boiled some rice as a main dish in the evening, but she always brought my plate to the table with a small piece of meat on it, and nothing else. I had begun the meal with eggplant salad, and I did not really mind. Sometimes I began with an artichoke, but I had been, for one distant year in my childhood, on an exclusive diet of artichokes, and have only recently become completely reconciled to them. It was the eggplant salad I loved. I was so attuned to its taste that I could tell a completely fresh one from a half-day-old one, and could barely touch the one that had spent the night in the icebox — perhaps because Boubinka refused to cover the food, considering it unnecessary. She made good dressings for all her salads, including the green ones. She was very involved with food, and hated women who smoked. She bought one pack of cigarettes at a time for my mother, revulsion written all over her face, and kept it for emergencies, locked up in a drawer.

As I said, she shopped every day, and on Saturdays, or on days when I was recovering from a cold and had not gone to school, I accompanied her. She loved to cook for me, but not for my friends. Her price was exclusivity, and I had long ago made my choice.

She carried all her shopping home herself. The idea of having something delivered seemed never to have entered her head, but I imagine now that she was afraid of substitution. She grew smaller with age, but never did she look as small as when she walked home, burdened, from market. She carried all her shopping in prosaic, brown paper shopping bags, which she poetically called, in Russian, "baskets." Furtive, slow, triumphant, and stooped, she moved along Madison Avenue as if her bags contained plunder filched from the depths of a pogrom. My offer to help was never accepted. "No," she said irrevocably, "you have other things to do." What those other things were was never made quite clear. But I do know that while we walked to and from the market, she counted on me to keep my eyes on the pavement and concentrate. Her eyes were not bad, just weakened with age, but mine were corrected to perfection, and she expected me to see what she might have missed. She hunted for treasure. It was a sport like any other, but it proved, over the years, to be extremely unrewarding. This didn't matter, because she hunted solely for pleasure. I think that if she had found what she was looking for, the total simplicity, the very beauty of her aim would have been destroyed. She hunted for diamonds — set or unset, she never specified. Had she found one, how sad and pedestrian would have been the day. Imagine having to call the police or put an ad in the newspaper. Fortunately, we never came to that. But how often I heard her say, "There, there!" How often I bent down, my heart beating fast, to pick up a diamond, only to find that it was glass backed with gold dust. How often I pounced on a pearl that had never seen the inside of an oyster. Once, I saw Boubinka set down her "baskets" in order to examine a thin platinum ring that had lost its stone. "Almost," she said, without a trace of disappointment, as she put it in her pocket. We kept them all — the "diamonds," the "pearls," and the thin platinum setting without a stone — and we brought them all home.

My mother's jewels, when my mother was away, were kept by my grandmother in the sugar canister, or in the coffee jar, or in the box of dry biscuits. Wrapped in handkerchiefs, one for the jades, another for the sapphires, a third for the chains and the bracelets and the old Cartier watch that needed to be repaired and never was, the jewels lay buried in edible innocence. They were quite safe, because Boubinka, apart from her daily shopping trip, was always home. And I saw the first signs of her failing memory the day she walked from the kitchen cupboard, where she kept the coffee jar, to a shelved closet (where the canned goods were, the jams, and the box of dry biscuits) next to my bedroom, and back to the kitchen cupboard again, looking for my mother's jewels.

✻

"What do you want to eat tonight?"

"Oh, anything. Anything you have. I'm not hungry."

"Why were you on the phone so long?"

"Oh, I don't know. I was talking to . . . a friend."

Her memory had begun to fail, and her health, too. She moved slowly now, from the kitchen to the living room, where we ate and where she slept, and between us conversation languished. She sat very straight in her chair by the dining table, with her hands folded in her lap. She no longer raised her index finger to her temple. She no longer said, "Think of that." Months and years went by, during which she did not mention acacias. She sat in silence, engrossed in memories that would, or could, no longer be shared.

Now we even separated for the summer. I went to visit friends. One summer I acted, but mostly washed dishes, in a stock company up in Massachusetts, and Boubinka stayed in New York. She no longer wanted to sit in a row with a lot of other Russian ladies who rocked their memories of the Black Sea on a porch facing Long Island Sound, and I had outgrown both them and the Russian pension, where the present never interrupted the past, save once, when a lady from Tiflis who was just this side of the change of life decided to have a hysterical pregnancy. I did not look back on those summers with any bitterness; they had been mine to read and dream in, to collect ladybugs in matchboxes, to play Ping-Pong with the sons and daughters of the Russian ladies. The younger generation came on Sunday afternoon, and sat around and yawned. I fell in love, hopelessly, with an uncouth, athletic Russian youth who stayed a whole week and sang "Two Guitars" after supper, by public request, and the Russian ladies wept. I swam — no, *we* swam, for Boubinka still went into the water in a decorous, black, cotton bathing suit that reached just below her knees and that I had helped her sew. Boubinka waded deeper and deeper, and when she got out of her depth she wrinkled her nose and began to dog-paddle, while I stood in the water and watched her and giggled. We began our meals with eggplant orientale, which I loved even more than my grandmother's eggplant salad. It was baked with tomatoes and olive oil, like moussaka, but it contained no meat. Eggplant orientale, after a winter of Boubinka's eggplant salad, was strangely festive, like roast chicken with a design of diamond-shaped truffles down its back after a steady diet of *poule-au-pot*. But I was lonely. Once, I made friends with a fisherman from Islip, and he gave me a turtle. (Again no symbolism, please.) He took me fishing a couple of times, but my pleasure was dampened by the sight of my grandmother and the Russian ladies, all in a row, watching us from the porch through pince-nez and binoculars.

This was a repetition of an earlier scene. When I was three and staying with her in a dreary provincial pension somewhere in France, I made friends with Primo Carnera. In fact, I adored him. And he was not unwilling to take me for a daily walk around the garden, while Boubinka watched us from the balcony of our room. Years later she said, "You don't remember his hands, but they should have belonged to an elephant, and the first time he went off with you, and took your hand, God! What a fright I had!"

Now my grandmother sat in her chair, living in a past that could no longer reach me, now that I had begun to live for the future. It was as if every single thing that could be said had been said.

She came to my wedding looking strangely poker faced, but she kept my December bouquet of lilies of the valley, and called my John her Johnchik, and so a new life began. I came to see her with a new baby, and eventually with another, and nobody knows what language she spoke to the boys, or they to her, but she kept very quiet while they felt the wrinkles on her face and the knotted veins on her hands.

One day, she was struck — very lightly — by a bus. After that she never went out. One night, when my mother was away, she fell, and could not get up off the floor until morning. She telephoned me and I came to her, but she could not explain what had happened. And soon after that, or long after that — I don't really remember — I rode downtown with her in an ambulance, until, with a diminishing wail of the siren, we stopped in front of the entrance to a nursing home.

*

Slowly, a new world takes precedence over the old. The past fades, memory melts, time collapses. The nurse is her mother, the nurse is her child — it is hard to tell which. They touch each other, like mother, like child, and it is by their touch that I can tell, at any given time, who plays mother, who plays child. "Mama," the nurse calls her. "Mama," she calls back. This one is her favorite. She is beautiful, coffee brown, and all round: round eyes, round nose, round eyebrows, round cheekbones. Her smile is lazy and small. She is faultless, with the patience of an angel. I promise her my seal parka, but she'll have to wait; I'm not hard on my clothes. My grandmother no longer attempts to speak English, and the French has disappeared from her Russian. To the nurse, she speaks in eloquent mime.

"Yes, Mama," answers the nurse.

It snows outside, but no one cares. It might as well be snowing in one of those glass paperweights with the Eiffel Tower inside, for all it matters around here. The world outside is unreal, it is past, it has ceased to exist, it is no longer necessary. No one will ever want to go out into the snow again. The woman who does not take her eyes off me, and smiles when I nod, is blind. The woman by the window picks at the pink blanket that covers her knees: pick, pick, pick. Her nails are lacquered and long, and I wonder who takes the time to give her a manicure. Tomorrow and the day after, I will find her, indefatigable as Penelope, at her useless, meaningful labor. Something falls to the ground with a dry snap. I have heard that sound before. It is the handle of Boubinka's umbrella, on the set of *First and Only Love Betrayed*. No, it's not an umbrella, it's a cane, and it belongs to the woman who is blind. I run to pick it up. The woman gropes for the handle and looks at me, annoyed. My grandmother's eyes follow me wherever I go, but her head does not move. She does not like me to speak to anybody, or to pick up a cane when it falls.

She lies in bed, and the bed has bars like a crib. She is very wasted. Her right hand that gripped the string handles of so many "baskets" is more gnarled than the left. As she sits up with great difficulty, I notice that her right shoulder is a good deal lower than her left. For many years, I have watched her eyelashes grow shorter, until suddenly now the eyelids are bare, and the eyes, unshaded, their pupils rimmed in black, their irises still gray-blue, hardly faded, but flecked with more yellow and white, watch me attentively, with a new-found coldness.

"Why did you curl your hair?" she asks.

"I didn't. I washed it this morning, and then I put it in very large rollers, so the ends won't look too ragged. I need a haircut."

We speak Russian together, as we always have, delighted to be able to exclude everybody from the conversation. But we no longer exclude anybody, because we include so little of ourselves. I can hear my own voice, as I did last night in a dream, and I do not like the sound of it. I find a comb in my bag and escape to the bathroom, which I note with satisfaction is kept admirably clean. I want to escape her unblinking scrutiny. My hair, in the bathroom mirror, looks straight. The snow took care of whatever I attempted to do to it this morning.

"Now my hair is straight, see?"

"It's not straight, and you don't have the face for curly hair."

Many years ago, she put my hair in curlers every night of the week. With infinite patience, because it was very fine hair with a tendency to slip, she wound it into rags, which she tore from old sheets. I went through printed sheets, pink sheets, white sheets. The rags were soft, but still it was hard to sleep on them, and when I called to her in the middle of the night and asked her to undo them, she always turned around and went back to her bed, saying, with an abominable accent, "Pour être belle il faut souffrir."

Well, I suffered, and now my hair is straight, and still I suffer, because she says it isn't. Mostly because she wants to disapprove. She watches me, appraises me, and there is no doubt she does not like what she sees. But why? Because I am an intruder. The new world has taken precedence over the old. When her favorite nurse walks in, she smiles.

At times, she returns to the family she has not seen in at least forty years. She takes them, she leaves them, but she does not exclude me. She asks me to give her regards to her sister. A moment later, a look of pain comes into her eyes. She remembers that her sister remained in Russia, and that I have never met her. She cries softly, like a child, and I hand her a Kleenex.

"Ah, thank you," she says. "You see, I forget. It's a curse

to live so long, so terribly long that it becomes impossible to remember."

The past moves up to the present, but the present is already part of a nonexistent future. Time refuses to be the slave of her capricious thoughts. It goes and escapes her.

So that her final world is timeless. At moments, it can be very dark, with occasional illuminations that are as unreal as fireworks. Boubinka looks worried: the nurses are plotting; they want to put her to death. A few minutes later, one of the accused nurses walks by, and Boubinka intercepts her with an impeccable smile.

She looks much calmer now; she sits in a chair by her bed, with a rug across her knees. She is smaller than she was last week.

"Comb my hair," she says, and adds, "It must look terrible."

It was cut when she could no longer manage her chignon at home by herself. Slowly, I comb out her hair. I do it slowly because it seems to soothe her. Her hair is curly, shiny, resilient, soft, warm, and brown. It smells of 4711. I find that hair hard to believe. She must be over ninety — for years she pretended to have forgotten the date of her birth, until in the end she actually did forget it — and her temples are only now beginning to go gray.

I tell her, "I must go; I promised the children."

"Yes, your children. Of course. And don't forget to give my love to Volodya."

"You mean John. Volodya was my father. He died years ago, remember?"

"Yes, of course. Johnchik. Our Johnchik. How could I forget our Johnchik. As I once said, it is a curse to live so long."

I kiss her forehead, and walk out without looking back.

Downstairs, in a large room, an old man sits at the piano, an old woman sings; another switches the television on and off. The scene is no drearier than it would be anywhere else where the green walls need painting, the piano tuning, the television repairing; and the singer's voice was never any good anyway. My grandmother is no longer wheeled down here. When I return, I shall find her in bed, or perhaps, if she does well, in her chair, with a rug across her knees, looking still smaller.

I want to trade this snow for another. I am going to Switzerland to ski. I shall be gone for a month, and in that other snow I will remember the grandmother of my Swiss boarding-school days, climbing, climbing, then resting, out of breath, then shouting, smiling, and waving her cane as I go down past her on my skis.

I have not told her that I am going away. I combed out her hair, and she kissed the back of my hand. Outside, the snow is deep; I see no taxi. I think, Surely she will wait for me.

✦

But she didn't. I received the news of her death in a sunny hotel room as I was packing my suitcase for the return trip. (She had never been one to interfere.) I took the chartered flight back as planned, and arrived in time to bury her.

The moment my mother asked me to go see Boubinka in the funeral chapel, there rose in my mind that insurmountable and immaterial structure that sometimes stands between the will and the accomplishment of an act. I should have obeyed instinct. Instead, I went duty's way, and made an irreparable mistake. I went, for the first time since my wedding, with a bouquet in my hand. I had made it of four immense carnations that were the color of tea roses and wax. I had cut their stems, and tied them closely to look like one. As I entered the funeral chapel, my hand shook, as it had with the lilies of the valley. I had never seen a dead person before. I was frightened, but pointlessly, because it wasn't Boubinka. Her face did not look wasted. It was heavily powdered — she who had never put anything on her face. The painful knotted veins on her hands seemed to have receded into the skin; the hands themselves were the color of the tea-rose carnations I placed next to them. Only the sight of the familiar wart on the side of her nose, which no human effort could efface, gave me a momentary start of pain. The moment was short and passed when I looked up and saw that the set of *The Last Farewells,* the only set I had not imagined, was the most unreal of them all, the most disturbing, and the least moving — because the sight of my grandmother in her coffin, surrounded by long flowers with wires running along their stems, could only shatter my present feeling for her, which was already a part of my memory, continuous, complex, and abstract.

And where was her old black dress, printed with almost microscopic and indecipherable flowers? Where was the pin I had secretly coveted throughout my childhood — a gold and diamond pansy with two baroque sapphire petals? She wore black satin with long sleeves and a little white lace around the neck (a deferential bow from the funeral chapel to her great age), pinned with a cameo that must have cost twenty-five cents. A failure in human taste had thought it necessary to remedy the purity of death with a semblance of art, and an image was realized that was not unlike that work of Arthur G. Dove (*Grandmother. Collage of shingles, needlepoint, page from the Concordance, pressed flowers*), from which I have always fled in distress.

People came, people went. They consoled my tearful

mother, but nobody said a word to me, and they were right not to, because I had long ago been reconciled to her death. She had died so many times. The first time, when she couldn't find my mother's jewels; the time she fell and couldn't tell me what exactly had happened; the time she called my husband by my father's name. And also, I suppose, because I looked all wrong for a funeral — dry eyed, with a kerchief over my head, and my face sunburned the color of ripe apricots. A man spoke. He had never seen my grandmother, of course, and so he did not speak of her finger-to-the-temple gesture, of our interminable white nights, of her orchid ball dress, of our exclusive love, of acacias, of our diamond-hunting on Madison Avenue. But why go on with this? We rode to the cemetery like gangsters, in a silent licorice limousine. We buried her, and I could not take my eyes off a carpet of plastic grass that covered the freshly dug grave. We buried her, and I have never gone back to the cemetery, and I don't know that I ever will.

*

The curtain is down, but I have not struck one of the sets. The truth is, I have buried my Boubinka on the set of the acacia trees, but we are not on the wide avenue in Odessa, we are in the country; we have grass, pale and darker, infinitely shaded, real. Who can measure the amount of good one human being does in this world? For years, for many of my helpless years, she *was* my whole world.

What Sadness

NICOLAS WAS on the telephone. I could not hear what
Jean-Loup said, but Nicolas said, very softly, "Good-
bye, Jean-Loup," and burst into tears.

Nicolas is seven and a half and quite small. But his eyes
are enormous, with mottled irises (sky and navy blue, lus-
trous, deep, brilliant, and multifaceted, like the backs of
trouts). His hair is dark blond, straight, and long, and always falls into his eyes.

Nicolas has a bed built like a sailor's bunk, with four
drawers underneath it. The drawers are large and deep, and
his three-and-a-half-year-old brother, Alex, could sleep in one
of them.

Nicolas, weeping loudly, chinned himself on the rim of
his bed, climbed in, and settled himself on his stomach. I
saw him quiver under the blanket toward the bottom of the
bed until the sound of his weeping became muffled. I un-
covered his head and spoke to his hair.

"Don't cry," I said.

"You should talk."

"Who do you think you're talking to?"

"You," he said.

"You have no right to speak to your mother that way. And stop crying. Listen: my best friend lives in Paris, and I live in New York, and it doesn't matter at all. I go there sometimes, and sometimes she comes here, and in between we write letters, and we still love each other very much, and we're still friends."

"You should talk," said Nicolas.

"Stop it," I said.

"Well, you and Daddy have money in the bank, so you can get on a plane when you want to, but what am I to do? I had ten dollars in my safe" — here Nicolas moaned, and guilt enveloped me like a folding parachute — "I had ten dollars, and I owed Daddy two, and you borrowed the rest."

"Nicolas, I don't like you to speak about money. Tomorrow is Monday. I'll go to the bank and get you your eight dollars back."

"And tomorrow, Monday, Jean-Loup is going to Paris on the boat."

Nicolas has a way of evoking a scene without having to describe it. I saw it all. I saw the funnel and heard the horn of the *Flandre*. And there, off-season, somewhere on deck, lightly dressed because he is not sensitive to cold, and waving good-bye to his brother Claude, stood Jean-Loup.

*

On Sunday morning (but that was only yesterday) Jean-Loup came to say good-bye. He stood in the middle of the white photographic studio (white walls, white floor, and white ceiling), dressed in a dark suit and black shoes, looking older than his twenty-one years. Claude was with him. Claude had just arrived from Paris, and was to take over

Jean-Loup's apartment. Jean-Loup introduced me to Claude, and Claude kissed my hand. The children said how do you do, but Alex looked at the skylight while he shook Claude's hand.

I turned to Jean-Loup. "I'm sorry that John is away, and that we can't all wish you good-bye together." I turned to Claude. "John is my husband."

"Yes, yes, I know," said Claude.

It was obvious that I did not know what I was saying. I turned back to Jean-Loup. "I saw your old shoes in the garbage can."

Nobody said anything.

"Quelle tristesse!" I finally said, with a sigh, making the transition for Jean-Loup, because, all the time that he had worked with John in the studio (a year and a half, to be exact), I had spoken mostly English to him, because I thought he should learn it well, and he had spoken mostly French to me.

"Ah, oui, Madame," said Jean-Loup. "C'est bien triste."

"Mais vous allez bien manger sur le *Flandre,* Jean-Loup."

"Et boire, Madame."

Claude wanted some instant coffee: instant because they were in a hurry. I went into the kitchen, which is contiguous to the studio, quickly brought the water to a boil, and made two cups. Then the three of us sat in silence in the middle of the empty, tidy studio. Quietly, at the back, the boys played boats with two dollies.

After a while, Jean-Loup looked around him and said, "Ça, au moins, je laisse le studio propre."

After that, Claude did all the talking. He looked very smart. Brown suit, hazel eyes, knitted tie to match the eyes, and tiny feet in Italian shoes. He spoke of the law (he is a barrister), of photographers' models, sports cars in traffic,

and Givenchy. Jean-Loup listened attentively and said
nothing. But then Jean-Loup rarely opens his mouth, except to say essential things like "The butter, please," or "Je
suis désolé de vous déranger, Madame, surtout que je sais
que vous êtes au travail, mais est-ce-que vous auriez par
hasard un Band-Aid?"

*

Jean-Loup had never once been late to work — not once in
a year and a half. The job of assistant to a photographer has
a vague beginning, perhaps, but no appreciable end. Nothing Jean-Loup was ever asked to do, or volunteered to do,
was too small or difficult for him. The house is large and
rather strange. People walk in and out of it as if it were
a windmill. The children live on one floor, John and I sleep
on another; there is a kitchen downstairs and another one
upstairs, and the studio is sixty feet long. There is little
peace. Jean-Loup answered the doorbell, shoveled snow,
accepted groceries and put them in the icebox, climbed step-
ladders to fit bulbs into sockets, and hurried to the post office
on his scooter because we were running low on airmail
stamps. All of which had nothing to do with his job. The
children always called on him when they wanted something. He built them each a bulletin board. He made a wire-
mesh cover for the terrarium where the chameleons live —
Camille, a sleepy female, and Leon, her mate. The children
got into the habit of whispering to Jean-Loup, and he always
crouched when he listened to them. Nicolas read the time
on Jean-Loup's large, round, silver watch, and Alex liked
to hold it against his ear. Everybody was delighted with
Jean-Loup — John, the agent, even the account executive
who arrived at the studio early one morning with a Waring
Blendor and immediately made himself a daiquiri. When

he fumbled his way down the stairs at lunchtime, he turned around on the landing and shouted, "Great guy, that French boy you have working for you." John complained to me once, "Jean-Loup was a little off today; I think he must be in love." But then the girl went back to France the next day, and so that was that.

Our relationship, Jean-Loup's and mine, was very simple, and I had never thought about it much until today. Jean-Loup would walk into the kitchen to return a prop, borrow a vase, or find a glass of water in which to dissolve two tablets of Alka-Seltzer. Often I forgot to lock the door, and most of the time he forgot to knock. Three days ago he walked in, and there I was, in my nightgown and bare feet, stalking the one small creature that had outwitted the exterminator. But Jean-Loup's incredible politeness immediately canceled all ridicule.

"Ah, pardon, Madame, ça, vraiment, je suis désolé . . ."

*

Jean-Loup and Claude finished their coffee, and then Jean-Loup went into the models' dressing room to try on the sweater I had bought for him. It was a bit loud, all in tones of blue, and the pattern was perhaps too complicated. I knew that Jean-Loup was of two minds about it, but then it fitted him perfectly, and would look well against a French landscape. I thought of the French countryside when I bought it for him, because Jean-Loup always carries next to his heart a photograph of his parents' country house, which was once the hunting lodge of the Château de Chenonceaux.

Wearing his sweater, Jean-Loup came toward me, and I told him he looked fine.

"Madame," he said, "je suis touché. Je suis ému." He

put his hands on my shoulders, and kissed me gently on both cheeks.

I put jackets on the children, and the five of us went down Fifth Avenue in a taxi. We parted at the entrance to the zoo. The children and I stood on the curb and waved, while Claude and Jean-Loup drove on. Nicolas seemed unconcerned, but then it's hard to tell about Nicolas. Alex shouted after the taxi, "Come back tomorrow!"

*

That evening (but that was last night), the telephone rang. I was reading to Nicolas, and he sighed when I put the book down to answer it.

It was Jean-Loup. "Madame, je voulais vous dire au revoir une dernière fois." There was a great deal of background noise that sounded as if it came from El Morocco. I no longer had the heart to speak English.

"Comme c'est gentil, Jean-Loup."

"Madame, je voulais vous . . ."

"Mais voyons, Jean-Loup."

Nicolas, who had jumped out of bed, tugged at the wire. "Ma, I want to say good-bye to Jean-Loup . . . Jean-Loup," said Nicolas sadly into the receiver.

I still don't know what Jean-Loup said to Nicolas. Nicolas answered in monosyllables. And it was then that he said "Good-bye, Jean-Loup" so touchingly, and burst into tears. Three quarters of an hour afterward, he was still inconsolable. I called Jean-Loup's apartment when it occurred to me suddenly that the sounds of El Morocco might have been recorded.

"Jean-Loup?"

"Madame?"

"Jean-Loup, je vous en prie. Nicolas est inconsolable. Soyez gentil. Dites-lui quelque chose. Dites-lui que vous allez essayer de revenir."

They had a long conversation, longer than I usually allow. It was a monologue, really, because Nicolas was silent; then, after a long while, he handed me the receiver.

"Madame," said Jean-Loup, and immediately I knew that he had been crying. "J'arrive. Je viens dire au revoir à Nicolas."

"Mais, Jean-Loup, voyons, mais vous avez déjà dit . . . Jean-Loup, je vous en prie. Il est tard. Jean-Loup . . ."

"Non, non, Madame, rien à faire. J'arrive."

❋

Nicolas climbed back into his bed. Alex moaned and turned around in his sleep. I closed the door to his room. Then the doorbell rang, and I had a vision of Jean-Loup's key, lying surrendered on John's desk. Jean-Loup came up the stairs very slowly, followed by a young, pale blonde. She was quite décolleté, and wholesome, in spite of her paleness. Her eyes were heavily drawn with brown pencil, but her mouth was painted with nothing more than a touch of lip gloss.

"I wanted to meet Nicolas," she said and shook my hand. She had a boy's handshake.

Jean-Loup walked toward Nicolas' bed and sat down on the chair I handed him. He stroked Nicolas' hair for a moment, then he put his face in his hands and began to cry. The girl stepped forward and put her hand on Nicolas' hair. It was a pretty hand, well cared for, with nails lacquered the color of ripe peaches.

"Il a de beaux cheveux," she said, and I noticed a slight

Italian accent that had escaped me when she spoke English. We stood there, she and I, looking at each other — I in my bare feet and chino pants and Lacoste shirt, and she in her short black silk — and we smiled. But Jean-Loup wept quietly with his forearms on the edge of Nicolas' bed.

"Mais voyons, Jean-Loup."

"Madame — " he started, but could not go on. I saw him put his hand in his pocket and quickly take out his silver watch. He hid it under Nicolas' pillow. Nicolas lifted his nose from the mattress, moved the pillow, and closed his hand over the watch.

"Jean-Loup, ne faites pas ça. Il est trop jeune."

"Non, non, Madame," said Jean-Loup from between his hands, "non, non, vous savez, Nicolas, c'est comme un fils pour moi. Non, laissez."

Then he got up and walked toward Alex's room. The girl looked at me. I nodded, and she followed him. In the half darkness, Jean-Loup bent down over Alex's bunk. Alex turned around in his sleep and found a pacifier with the tip of his nose. He moved his head slightly, and snapped it up as a chameleon snaps up a fly. The girl laughed. Jean-Loup, his eyelashes lowered, his features sealed, suddenly, by the dim night-light, brought his finger to his lips in the perpetual gesture of Redon's *Silence*.

On the landing, just as he was about to go down the stairs, Jean-Loup turned around and fell into my arms. He was tall and smelled of Scotch and cigarettes, but he felt like a child.

"Madame," he said, with his head on my shoulder, "je veux vous . . ."

"Jean-Loup, je vous en prie . . ."

"Je suis si attaché aux enfants, Madame, et John, avec moi . . . Enfin, c'est rare, tout ça, dans la vie . . ."

"Jean-Loup," I said, hesitating a little, "est-ce-que vous aviez des invités, chez vous?"

"Oui, Madame."

"Alors, filez, filez."

*

Nicolas went to sleep on his back, which only happens when he battles sleep until it overwhelms him suddenly, and the watch lay face down by his open right hand, as if it had spilled out of it — which it had. And I felt as if time had moved back, away from the subtlety, the complexity, the urbanity of most contemporary human situations. (Those situations that are discussed over the telephone too late at night, or over drinks too early in the day.) The plotted story of Jean-Loup in America was so simple it was almost an affront; the clichés, like beads, followed one another evenly. It was not unlike the obsolescent plot of the latest Soviet film. Let me tell *its* beads: the film opens on a field of wheat; a man's voice says, "He died a hero, far from his village, and strangers put flowers on his grave." (And I say to myself, How dare they?) Then a flashback: we see the hero's mother; she works in the fields; her son is at the front; he is nineteen and handsome, and a moment later, all by himself, he knocks out two tanks; thus he obtains leave to see his mother and repair the roof of their house. On the train he meets the heroine; she is ravishingly healthy and big boned (look at those wrists); moreover, she is able to sit up in a wagonload of hay and ask the hero with passionate sincerity, "Do you believe in the power of friendship?" I smile, but little by little, eroded by all this unashamed simplicity (by the sight of the mother running through her field of wheat to embrace the son who will soon die), my defenses crumble. I can't bear it; yet I love it. I love to be moved, as I am now moved (mercifully, this is life, not a film) about Jean-Loup, who had come from the Old Country to the New World, to serve his apprenticeship. He was young, he worked hard, he learned a lot. And then one day his visa expired and he could not get it renewed. ("How can a government be so cruel?" asks Nicolas.) He had been happy here, and he had become attached to us all. We did not want him to go, and he didn't want to go. But he had to. He had to start on his own. And become a man.

❋

It is early afternoon. Jean-Loup sailed this morning. The house, the studio especially, is filled with his presence. The mail brought no news of John. I sit on my bed and write. Nicolas is at my desk with his safe, and counts his money on his fingers. Alex, on the floor by my bedside, plays with a Mercedes and a Porsche. It is storming out and my pencil needs sharpening. Nicolas has given me his silver watch for safekeeping — from Alex, whom he has lately christened Highway Robbery. I keep it by my bedside, and now, on its large white face, I see the delicate second hand, as intricately constructed as a chameleon's paw, move forward imperceptibly.

Grief

Was it summer? Was it spring or was it fall? One window of the living room was open. It was warm enough, at any rate, for that window to be open, but it was not really warm.

Down below, at the corner, a Madison Avenue bus came to a stop. The doors wheezed open, the nickels clanked down their steel chutes. A momentary silence, and then my grandmother screamed.

She sat in a rocking chair by the window, head thrown back, both hands holding her head, the right one tightened into a fist crumpled over a handkerchief.

She screamed again.

Niobe, I thought. Wounded Niobe. Thermae Museum. Rome. Fifth century. The good century, but late fifth, the teacher had said, because the drapery that covered the lower part of the body was on the verge of becoming opaque. I was very involved with history of art at the time, and even more involved with the Egyptians than I was with the Greeks, but there was nothing of the classroom in that moment, except that I sat cross-legged at my grandmother's feet like the scribe in the Cairo Museum, and kept my mind crowded with all this irrelevant, or relevant, information, because I did not want to think about my grandmother.

Grief has an economy of movement, a sparseness valid from the beginning, and, I suppose, to the end, of time. Under the thin black dress my grandmother wore, I could see the strain, the terrible pain in her body — a pain that was not physical and that I had never seen before.

Why was I home and not in school? Did I have a cold or was it Saturday?

The doors of the bus wheezed shut and off it went. Then came the sound of hoofs: the mounted police, either coming from or going to the armory across the avenue.

My grandmother rocked, quite violently, in silence. I watched her legs and feet and, more particularly, her slippers. They were of patterned felt, like the ones usually worn by French concierges. My grandmother had not told me about them. They seemed to be new. In fact, I had never seen them before. This was not the moment to ask, but I wondered where she had found them. The rocker squeaked slightly, back and forth, back and forth. I thought that later, much later, I would oil it with the oil we used for the sewing machine.

As my grandmother continued to rock, the letter that lay folded in her lap slid off, silently, and lay, still folded, at her feet. I did not move to pick it up. When she rocked all the way back, her feet in their concierge slippers came off the ground. I could see that the letter, a single sheet of airmail paper covered on both sides, was in Russian. To think that I had bothered to go downstairs to get that letter, that I had unlocked and locked the mailbox, that I had brought it up and given it to her.

The hand that held the handkerchief came to rest in my

grandmother's lap, taking the place of the letter. Her fist tightened, and she moaned, just once. She still continued to rock; her left hand still held her head, the elbow at a sharp angle, the only corner in that otherwise perfect circle of despair.

Another bus came and went, and took forever, it seemed; and I kept wondering if I should shut the window. Before I could make up my mind, my grandmother spoke, and the voice that came out of her was not her own. I had heard of mediums, and trances, and mediums in trances, but I did not know that my grandmother, whose voice was usually light and held little depth, could suddenly turn into a dark contralto.

"Burned. My children. *Burned!*" she said, or shouted, or screamed, in that newly found voice; it was hard to tell what she was doing, the sound of her was so foreign to me. And then her left hand fell into her lap.

"Burned," she said once more, and was silent. The rocker, poised all the way back, stood suspended for a moment and moved forward again. It was then that I understood, and panic gripped me — not by the throat, but by the spine, somewhere along my back. It rose to the top of my head, only to descend, past a strangely sexual moment, until I could feel it reach the very tips of my toes. And I knew that it would be a long time before I would close the window, a long time before I would move at all.

Would my grandmother have behaved — more or less — as she did had I not been in the room? It is hard to tell. The line dividing truth from drama is weaker than the one that separates acting in public (even before an audience of one) and reacting in solitude. Besides, my grandmother was Russian.

❋

She must have been in her early seventies at the time. It is impossible to remember exactly, because she was always so vague about her age. Once, when I questioned her directly, she answered — in the offhand way she had of answering when she was either evading or else not telling the truth — that she did not really know how old she was. She had lost her birth certificate in some pogrom or other, and now she no longer had a point of reference.

I remember clearly that I was fifteen, and that all the arrangements between my grandmother and myself, including our respective ages, had suited me to perfection until a few moments before, when they had become untenably reversed.

Did an hour go by or just enough time to sigh a sigh? It is hard to tell. I kept thinking, Why did she say "Burned"? That, in itself, in the end, seemed unimportant. I bent forward and picked up the folded letter. My grandmother's eyes were closed; she did not see me. The word "Auschwitz" written in the Roman alphabet seemed to lift itself from the first paragraph. I knew, from the time it had taken her, that she had been unable to read much beyond it. I did not bother to decipher the written Cyrillic, which, from lack of experience, I found so much harder to read than the printed alphabet. I put the folded letter in my pocket.

I remember an endless silence, and then I said, very firmly, "We shall have to tell my mother."

"No — no!" she screamed in that strange contralto. Her hands went up to her head again. The handkerchief, hopelessly rumpled and small, remained in her lap.

"Why not?" I asked.

She rocked herself, violently, slippers on and off the ground, and her voice, when it finally came, was on all sorts of different levels: it broke and stopped; and then it started again; and each time the pitch was different. This is what she said: "We can't. She's an artist — she's on tour — we must let her do what she's always done — play the piano — you mustn't interfere — she earns your living, mine — she's always earned everybody's living — oh, my children!" she said, and her slippers came to rest on the floor. "My poor children!"

*

I shut the window and made a telephone call. It never occurred to me to call a doctor, although my grandmother now sat back silent, gray, still, and almost lifeless. All I knew was that she was *not* sick. I called H——, a woman I admired and loved beyond any other, in the way that a child can only love and admire her best friend's mother. She was then an editor on the *New York Times,* and I thought that she would know what to do, where to turn, where to get help, and most important, it seemed, how to get news.

It must have been morning still, and not even late morning, because H—— came right away. She lived two blocks uptown from us, and she must have been about to go down to her office. She sat on the maroon couch by my grandmother's rocking chair, and crossed her legs, and smoked a cigarette. Did she actually smoke a cigarette? I think that she began to smoke much later, but when I try to remember, I find her on the maroon couch with her legs crossed, smoking. She wore a mannish suit of gray flannel (was it fall, then?) and a frilly white silk shirt, her mother's seed pearls, and a small jeweled coral-and-gold hand pinned to her jacket. I sat on the floor and watched her run a comb through her hair, put out her cigarette, cross and uncross her legs. They were lovely, and she wore bold net stockings, which very few women dared wear at the time, and brown crocodile sandals. (Perhaps it was spring, after all, because of the sandals.) Spring or fall, I thought, This day must pass, and I must stop sitting on the floor where one is inextricably faced with people's legs and feet. I wanted time to pass immediately, so that this day would become long ago and I would be old enough to wear net stockings and hit life head on.

H —— said there was nothing to be done that she could do here and now. She would try to get news. She would call later in the day. And then she was gone. And there was only my grandmother left, and I. Grandmother and I.

❋

My uncle was the only playmate of my early childhood. I cannot remember another. He was not a blood relation but the husband of my mother's sister. We all lived together — my mother, my grandmother, my aunt, my uncle, and a transient nurse for me — in a series of equivalent Paris apartments with little sun and long corridors. I managed the nurses, rather demonically. My mother was often absent. When she was not away, I see her bent over my crib or my bed, dressed in long satin. The train of the dress had a serpentine way of lingering in the crack of the door, and I hit the pillows reeking of Arpège. My mother, however, dressed at Lelong's. And, in the evening, all was plunging necklines and subdued satin, the shades leaning toward plum. Any further embellishment came separately, in the form of pearls and diamonds. Our only source of income was what my mother earned playing the piano. That's why she was away so much. I don't know how much my uncle contributed; I would rather not think about that.

The nurses I remember ruling with blackmail. "If you let me do that, I won't tell my grandmother that you . . ." My mother ruled me by her absences. My grandmother ruled by the force of her love. My aunt held no power, nor did my uncle, and I had none over them. They were my closest friends. They always lived at the end of a corridor.

My uncle had something to do with jewels. He kept precious and semiprecious stones folded away in the dead center of two thicknesses of white paper. First tissue paper (that one made a sound) and then thick paper (that one remained silent). The stones seemed small. They were of little value, probably. But, of course, they were magical.

My uncle had a pair of copper scales, exactly like the ones Justice holds but very small. The weights were minute, and my uncle let me weigh the stones. We played store. He would mark down the weight on large sheets of paper as I called it out; then he would think. Finally, he quoted a price. I bargained. He gave in. He wrapped the stone of my choice, and I could take it with me to my room. The envelope was quite flat. There was something written on it. It was not unlike the letter that my grandmother received toward the end of the Second World War.

My aunt was wide, gay, warm, funny, and prone to hysteria. At times I heard her screaming behind the closed door of her room. This did not happen very often, and there were long, calm stretches in between. I asked my grandmother an urgent set of questions. My grandmother hesitated; then she came right out with it and told me my aunt was rolling on the floor. She was in pain and couldn't help it; different people reacted differently to pain, and my aunt's way was to roll on the floor. My grandmother also said that it was nothing to worry about, and that it would only happen for a few hours at a time, perhaps a dozen times in a year. I adored my aunt. She loved to laugh and was always home. She had many women friends who came to see her and who kissed me, Russian fashion, on the mouth. This I did not like. I called my aunt Tutu (pronounced "Tyootyoo") and my uncle, Dudu ("Dyoodyoo").

One day Dudu and I were walking hand in hand by the Bourse. A persistent and distinct hum came from that building. It frightened me. I asked, "What are they doing in there?"

He said, "Killing each other."

I hurried him off.

Later, many years later, Dudu asked, "What single object, beyond any other, can improve a woman's face?"

"Love," I said, tentatively, because Dudu had used the word "object."

"*Entirely wrong!*" Dudu practically jumped on me, he was so angry. "The answer is *glasses!*"

I was about ten and had worn glasses before I was nine, and now I needed newer, thicker ones. I thought, Surely Dudu is trying to comfort me. But he wasn't. I suddenly realized that he wasn't. And at that moment, very coolly, affections and loyalties intact, I decided that Dudu must be slightly mad, or else mistaken, or else both at the same time.

＊

Suddenly I was eleven and packing to go to the States. I was going with my grandmother. My mother awaited us in New York. I looked forward to the *Ile de France* and to nothing else. I felt the war would come, because everyone spoke of little else.

I was putting neat piles of underwear into my suitcase, and Dudu sat on a small straight chair, facing the wrong way, watching me. He asked, "Supposing you found yourself in a city that was being bombed. Now, where would you go?"

"Into a shelter, of course."

"Wrong; all wrong, *entirely* wrong. Do you know what *I* would do? I would climb, or ride the elevator, to the very top of the very tallest building in that city, and sit down the way I am sitting right now, and await my fate."

At that point I sensed, for the first time in my life, a new kind of danger. It made me acutely uncomfortable. It was not physical danger — neither one of us was threatened; there was no imminent or even possible catastrophe in sight. And yet I felt that events might be *made* to happen by thought alone. And Dudu was not thinking correctly, I was quite sure of that. And I couldn't change his way of thinking. I wanted to pack him with my underwear so that I need never lose sight of him when he was thinking badly; but that was impossible, and so our parting had, for me, an added element of sadness.

＊

I opened the window of the compartment on the train that was to take my grandmother and me from Paris to Le Havre. We were in the Gare St-Lazare in the month of May, and I wore my mulberry wool coat, with velvet collar and buttons, and short white gloves. I opened the window and there was Tutu, standing just below me, on the platform. It was as if she stood in a hole. She tried to smile. And then the train started, and — horrors! — Tutu started off with it. She walked, she trotted, she cried. The train picked up speed, and so did Tutu; she was running full speed now, her face drenched with tears, while Dudu stood far behind, dim but straight as an exclamation mark through all the smoke. I waved, and then there was nothing left to do but to shut the window and sit down and sob and sob as if the end of life had come. My grandmother hid behind her handkerchief. "Stop it," she said.

"But I shall never see them again. *Never.*"

(Oh those fearful insights children have, and then refuse to acknowledge in their own children.)

"Your gloves are all sooty. So is your face." My grandmother blew into her handkerchief. "Take off your gloves," she said. Then, "Give me your handkerchief."

She did not have to spit into it. I closed my eyes, and she wiped my face with my tears.

*

Tutu was my mother's elder sister. My mother, the youngest of four, had come to Paris to study at the Conservatoire in 1912. She had two brothers. The older one — the charming, the promising, the irresistible one — perished in the margin of all his promises, killed in Siberia during the Russian Revolution. The other one, poor adolescent émigré, was left behind, in Paris, while my mother and my grandmother returned to Russia for a vacation in July 1914. They intended to stay a few weeks and became stranded there, first by war and then by revolution. My mother says that she never understood or questioned why her brother didn't come with them. He had a job, and perhaps that had something to do with it. Somehow, in 1917, he managed to rejoin them, and they all three went back to Paris in January of 1920.

This uncle, whose name was Jascha, grew to resemble the solitary representative of a species of small animal no pack in the forest would adopt. He never seemed to attack but was forever defending himself. He managed, but his code was his own; it wasn't mine, and it didn't seem to be anybody else's. Until a numerous assemblage of diseases — including the tuberculosis he contracted during the Occupation — finally killed him off at a respectable age, he always managed to survive.

When the Germans came in the spring of 1940, my uncle fled from Paris into the countryside. For a while he lived off wild plants, and roots, and the bark of trees. Or so he told me later. (He was a great teller of tales.) He wandered around the countryside, hid in forests, settled here and there for short, indefinite, safe periods, breaking his exile occasionally with short reconnaissance trips into Paris. In that way he survived the Occupation. But Tutu and Dudu did not. They died, gassed in Auschwitz.

Mercifully, there were no details either in the letter my resourceful uncle sent my grandmother, or through surviving friends, or through the Red Cross.

*

Did a week go by? Or two, or three? I think that my mother was on tour for about three weeks after the day my grandmother received the letter. Did I stay home, or go to school, or hover between the two? I must have gone to school at some point, because of something that happened. How did my grandmother and I sleep, eat, shop, cook? I do not remember. I remember moving silently through the rooms. My grandmother shuffled about in her slippers. The apartment was small, and neither one of us could get very far from the other. I remember the silence that appeared to envelop us both, a silence that had a strange effect on sound. It stifled the hoofs of the mounted police, throttled the noise of traffic (and particularly of the buses), smothered the telephone, muted our voices, and drowned laughter forever, it seemed. The rest is blank — the benevolent blank of blocked-out pain. Who took care of whom? I do not remember taking care of my grandmother. Yet she took no pills to reduce the range of her pain, no medicine to hinder the mind and make it forget long enough to permit sleep. I remember her silences, her slippers, and her wet handkerchiefs. When everything is still at night and I am alone, I can still hear her shuffling in her slippers.

Then, out of hopeless love for a boy most of the other girls in class (and I was one of them) also loved to distraction, a friend of mine threw herself out of the window of her parents' Madison Avenue apartment and landed on top of a bus. When she was put on the stretcher of the ambulance that was to take her to a hospital, she said, "Look, there is a run in my sock." And died. I did not tell my grandmother. So many people died before they were supposed to, for reasons I could — and yet could not — understand. I had only once had a glimpse of a possible reason: Dudu's irremediably faulty thinking. But it explained nothing. The violence around me terrified and pursued me. And I heard my grandmother shuffling in my dreams.

*

Eventually my mother returned. We could not have told her immediately, because I remember that when we did she was wearing a nightgown with a dressing gown over it. We had agreed that my grandmother was to tell her, and then I was to hand her the letter. My mother sat on the maroon couch, and my grandmother told her. My mother swayed forward a little; then she swayed back. But grief has a fatal economy of movement. All my mother did was what my grandmother had done before her. She put her hands up to her head, and then she screamed.

Chopin

IN THE STUDY, Guy Dutour, known to the village as *"notre cher Maître,"* played the Andante spianato, opus 22. When he began the Grande Polonaise brillante, his lap dog, Malachite, asleep on a cushion by the pedals, raised her heavy Pekinese head, opened her laminated idol's eyes one at a time, and wheezed appreciation. Upstairs, in the enormous bedroom madame de Sévigné had occupied as a girl, his young wife, Annette, examined the pale curve of her eyebrow in a magnifying mirror. She held no tweezers; she could no more touch a hair of her brow than pluck a straying blossom at the edge of the pond.

At the kitchen door, Guy Dutour's maid of fifteen years, Gertrude, heard the chef's bicycle on the graveled path. He dismounted with the bicycle still in motion, and Gertrude caught the handlebars like a bridle. Once he was over the threshold, she took off his beret and his trench coat, and handed him his chef's hat.

It had rained for two weeks now; sometimes it cleared toward the end of an afternoon, just long enough for the sun to illuminate the landscape until it looked like a page from *les Très Riches Heures,* and then it rained again. The water screws weltered in the drowned wild-strawberry beds, a fresh downpour tumbled the pink snails off the raspberry bushes, and the frogs were in paradise. The wind always came from the east, and on the far horizon four cypresses leaned to the right, like the first diligent strokes in a child's exercise book. Annette watched them from the window as she twisted her pale hair into a fan-shaped knot, in the manner of the peasant women of the county; then she turned to her back-view mirror to secure it, high, with two gold barrettes from Cartier's. In the study, Malachite lightly snored at the crescendos in the Mazurka, opus 24, no. 4. In the kitchen, the chef's right hand beat a rotary motion with a silver fork while his left squeezed olive oil from a medicine dropper. Then Gertrude announced lunch. *Œufs mayonnaise, escalopes de veau Maintenon, petits pois, laitue, fromage de chèvre, mousse au chocolat,* and coffee. Over coffee, Guy Dutour addressed his wife: "My dear, what are your plans for the afternoon?" And Annette answered, "A little sleep; perhaps a little read; then Gertrude is going to help me hang the full-length mirror. She is going to the post office to get my new Balenciaga. And I must supervise the dinner. Have you forgotten? We have guests tonight."

Once in the enormous bed and under the vicuña, Annette placed two small balls of hardened pink wax in the shells of her ears, to protect herself from the frogs, and fell into a sleep of fleeting, soundless visions. In the study, his slippered feet on the arm of the couch, Guy Dutour drowsed over Simenon's latest *Maigret.* At the kitchen table, propped by cushions, a napkin tied around her neck, Malachite ate cold chicken on Gertrude's left, while at the farm on the estate, Eglantine, the farmer's wife, in search of a truce with the flooded afternoon, fed her small twins *vin ordinaire* from a teaspoon before putting them to the breast. Drunk in the cellar, her husband, Pierre-Emile, sang and lamented his sinking vineyards as he rubbed Baume Bengué into the joints of his knees.

Guy Dutour was awakened by a little girl who moved toward him jerkily, her eyes strained, her face wet, delicate, and green. She held an offering of sweet peas in one hand and half a goat cheese in the other. Before she attempted the poem dedicated to *"notre cher Maître,"* Guy Dutour brought her to the cushion by the pedals and prodded her hand into a crescent of perfumed sleeping fur. Malachite opened one laminated eye, wheezed, growled, barked, and, in warning, bit the air sideways.

When Gertrude took away the sobbing little girl, Guy Dutour sat down to the piano and worked a passage from the Mazurka, opus 24, no. 4, with infinite patience, as if he were playing Czerny back in his sedulous childhood. Gertrude, her left hand on the doorknob, waited for the end of a phrase to bring in the chamomile tea. As she was about to set the cup and saucer on the rim of the piano, the teaspoon wavered, rattled, and fell to the carpetless floor. Gertrude laughed, and her direct laughter, urgent and uniting, settled between them like a conspiracy. For Guy Dutour, the moment (sprung from the fluid mazurka and his right shoulder blade, which ached from playing in the dampness) converged on Gertrude's back and her smell (fresh-chopped tarragon, delicate sweat, and a drop of *Eau de Javel*). He watched her wide back, stretching the blue lawn house dress as she bent to pick up the spoon, and he remembered and saw her climbing aboard trains with the mute practice keyboard — Gertrude, who never interrupted a phrase and saved his leftover chamomile to rinse her hair! The chilled longing, the stilled sadness of the mazurka still held to his fingertips as his hand gently went out to her; his insured hand, kissed so often, came down the length of her spine and — as she straightened, gripping her spoon — over the lenient flesh of her buttock.

Through it all, dressed in her new Balenciaga, Annette had stood in the doorway like one of those absurd apparitions summoned by Simenon to force an improbable dénouement.

Gertrude, who saw her in Guy Dutour's eyes, walked out of the room and made her way to the kitchen carefully, like a patient after adrenalin. Annette ran upstairs, combed out her pale hair, and put in a phone call to her lover in Paris. While waiting, she thought of her black sealskin coat, and decided that for the coming season its shoulders should be taken in a little. She imagined her other furs, labeled, hibernating in cold storage. She catalogued them, simultaneously wrapping the image of her husband in infinite tenderness. And she finished the list with the private little smile she had, at times, smiled against the lapel of a dinner jacket when a man, at a charity ball, complimented her on the skin of her back and shoulders. She canceled her call.

Guy Dutour had thrown a raincoat over his shoulders, tucked Malachite under his arm, and run slowly to the farmhouse, where he now sat drinking his third glass of Anjou rosé with Pierre-Emile while Eglantine rocked the twins, who slept, flushed and fitful, grasping for air with small mottled hands. In spite of her curiosity — she sniffed intrigue behind the unexpected visit — Eglantine often deserted the men's conversation to dream of a set of dentures patterned on Annette's small and delectable teeth.

Guy Dutour left them to run his long black Chrysler through the mud of the village; he crossed the swollen river, grazed and splashed the length of wall by the Manoir de Vivefontaine, drove through the brown countryside and into the forest, until he saw, posed like a white nest in a clearing, the Château de Cybèle. Malachite whined and trembled by the doorstep as Guy Dutour hesitated, then recognized the loose stone that the gatekeeper had shown him. Underneath it was a key. The door opened silently, and in spite of her wheeze, which had amplified with the damp drive and the new dust, Malachite followed Guy Dutour as he tried the easy marble staircase and haunted the forsaken rooms with the idea of renting, perhaps, for the following summer.

When he returned, Annette and her two guests, the lisping conductor and the New York impresario who never spoke, were sitting down to dinner. Gertrude served *asperges sauce mousseline, poulet à l'estragon, carottes au beurre noir,* and *chicorée à l'ail.* Eglantine, still in search of intrigue, made her daily delivery in person. "Good evening, ladies and gentlemen," she said as she slowly crossed the dining room, balancing a wet copy of *France-Soir* on her head; she carried the fresh goat cheese to the kitchen, that Gertrude might bring it back in. They had *crème renversée.* Throughout dinner, the conductor who lisped spoke: "My beat . . ." he said. "My baton . . ." "The way *I* handle a musician . . ." "My sinus will disappear, God forbid," he said, "the day I die." They took their coffee into the study, and Guy Dutour sat down to the piano. Malachite slept through the Andante spianato, opus 22, the Grande Polonaise brillante, and the Etude, opus 10, no. 4. "Marvelous!" said the New York impresario, over a large cup of *tilleul.* "Stupendous and stupefying!" said the lisping conductor, and, waving Guy Dutour aside, he got up, rubbed his jeweled hands together, walked toward the Pleyel, and sat down.

Annette excused herself and went upstairs. She called Gertrude to the enormous bedroom and asked for a pail of hot water. She took her habitual cool bath. Alone in the bed, having found with her feet the heat of one of three hot-water bottles, Annette lay still among the cornflowers of her printed linen sheets. But she did not sleep. There was an unexpected crescendo in the Etude, opus 10, no. 4, and the customary decrescendo of the chef's bicycle on the graveled path. There was the rain. There were frogs. There was the old beaver coat she wore in bad weather, which she would give Gertrude as a gesture. There was the dark mink she need no longer keep for the evenings, because now she would have the sables — the outrageous, snuff-colored sables, wild and more tender to the skin of her back than a man's dark love; the sable coat would now be hers because she had forgiven.

The Critic

B RAVO!" cried a piano student in the first row of Carnegie Hall.

"Braaa . . . vo!" cried a rival pianist in the third row, and he turned profile as he rose, hoping to be recognized.

Guy Dutour bowed.

A girl with a thin voice shouted in the balcony; in a second-tier box, an older woman, before tearing the gloves from her hands, adjusted her pince-nez in order to undo twenty-four pearl buttons; and Justin Berg, the critic, rose from an anonymous seat at the back of the orchestra, lit a Player's cigarette under the nearest EXIT sign, and disappeared, precipitato.

The applause moved toward Guy Dutour like a physical presence, and at the moment when he felt it touch him he bowed again, reverently, concisely.

On his platform, the conductor stood very still, smiling his absolute smile, clapping politely, until, in a sputter of gymnastics that sent chandelier reflections flying from his diamond rings, he descended, shook Guy Dutour's right hand in both of his, fell into step for their reciprocal bow, and whispered, lisping distinctly, into the pianist's left ear, "Splendid, splendid, we sizzled!"

Then, to the tempered beat of the orchestra's applause, the pianist and the conductor walked toward the wings, only to return, unite their bows, and mop their brows.

✻

While Guy Dutour was playing, his wife, Annette, young and pale and wearing her rose-printed Givenchy for the first time, opened the door of the soloist's greenroom a slit, reached out, and tapped on the attendant's shoulder with a frail, pink-tipped finger. He started and turned around, and she handed him a small florist's box. "Please rid me of this," she said, and smiled her private smile. "If you like, give it to your wife. I am afraid the contents would give Maître Dutour an attack of hay fever." She quickly closed the door in the face of a draft that carried a weak ricochet of cadenza, and returned, in a murmur of taffeta, to her corner of the leather couch. She sat down, arranged the folds of her skirt, and thought of that single rose she had been astonished to find in its nest of waxed green paper. A single, deeply scented, forced, dark red rose, and not the trace of a note. She retreated into Agatha Christie, and listened with one ear as the water came to a boil on an electric plate by the upright piano.

Wearing a faded blue house dress and a new pair of sneakers, Gertrude, Guy Dutour's maid for sixteen years, crept under the thin three-legged table to disconnect the current; then she busied herself with pinches of *tilleul* and a teapot. At the other end of the leather couch, Guy Dutour's impresario sighed and bent forward to lift a bottle from the floor. As he refilled his Dixie cup with Pommard

'45, Guy Dutour's Pekinese, Malachite, who was resting on her gros-point cushion by the window, inhaled a sudden misery of steaming radiator heat, opened her right eye to relinquish a tear, and exhaled slowly on a faint, hurt note — her chronic wheeze always exaggerated by the climatic hardships of the North American tour.

Of Beethoven's Piano Concerto no. 4 in G Major none of them had heard a note.

❋

When Guy Dutour, accompanied by the conductor, entered the soloist's greenroom, Annette lifted her bright blue eyes from the middle of a paragraph and said, "What a surprise! I did not expect you so quickly!" The conductor came toward her with great strides and broke in two as he bent to kiss the tiny violet vein that traveled the region behind her left ear. "Salut!" he said in the direction of Gertrude, who was about to feed Guy Dutour his cup of tisane. He skipped the impresario, since they were not, this season, on speaking terms. When he clapped shut the door of the conductor's greenroom — which was adjacent to the soloist's — he was greeted by his New York physician, who sat under a standing lamp, reading Bergson through bifocals rimmed more heavily than they need have been. "Ah! . . ." said the conductor, and he bowed deeply. "Maestro Cagliostro!" He took off his dinner jacket, liberated a heavy, gold-rope cuff link, rolled back his sleeve, and when he had found the nearest chair, sacrificed his right arm to the blood-pressure rites. The pump panted, and exhaled.

"Still treating Justin Berg?" asked the conductor.

❋

"Are you ready?" shouted Guy Dutour after he had changed, behind a screen, into a duplicate dinner jacket.

"Certainly not!" the conductor — who had packs up his nostrils — shouted back from his room, in a choked, de-nasalized voice.

Unwilling to wait any longer, Guy Dutour gave Gertrude the signal. Annette and the impresario rose, and Annette arranged the folds of her skirt. Gertrude knocked on the inside of the soloist's greenroom door. The attendant immediately opened it to admit — first in line as always — a very large woman dressed in black, a caryatid-in-mourning, the musician's friend and hostess: Wilena Samuels.

Guy Dutour was folded silently into her giant's arms while high above his shoulder she withdrew from her jet-beaded reticule a moist handkerchief round as a doily. When she released Guy Dutour, Annette moved into the circle of her arms and stood there, like the thin water-spout of a great fountain.

"Did Justin Berg sleep?" Annette asked.

*

Gertrude's evening having come to an end, she put on the old beaver coat Annette had given her the preceding summer, picked up Malachite and her cushion, and softly, in her sneakers, ran out of the room and down the steps of the Fifty-sixth Street entrance. As she waited for a taxi under the canopy, the magnificent doorman of the Balalaika waved at her from under his canopy, and she waved back with her free arm. A gentle snow traveled on the bias. Malachite sneezed. "We are going to the Hotel Carlyle!" Gertrude had memorized and now recited to the driver. When they stopped in front of the hotel, she cried, "Go back! Go back!" She had forgotten the suitcase with Guy

Dutour's clothes, his toilet articles, the electric plate, the teapot, and the box of *tilleul*.

*

Wilena Samuels' evening having just begun, small groups slowly formed under her paintings, some of which were reputed to be fakes. "Admirable!" said the eminent French biographer as he passed a suspect Juan Gris, to a couple walking in the opposite direction, who could not tell whether he had spoken English or French. "Naturellement, ce qui convient le mieux au tempérament de Maître Dutour, c'est 'Litz' et Chopin," he said, without being asked, to the next couple, whom he recognized as French because the woman gilded only the very tips of her hair, and the man, having discovered Space Shoes, had ordered them in patent leather for evening. Then he saw Guy Dutour coming toward him, framed by Wilena Samuels, who walked directly behind him. "A la santé de notre cher Maître," he added, "le musicien sans peur et sans reproche." And he raised, rather too high, his Venetian glass with a fluted stem. Wilena Samuels, aware of doom riding the air like escaping gas, introduced Guy Dutour to a tall English comedienne who stood appropriately by. He noted that she wore nothing under a confection of black velvet, which was slit to the knee; no jewels beyond an identical gold rope on each sun-tanned wrist; no ornaments save for a single, forced, deep red rose, pinned at the height of her Empire waist.

"Don't you hate critics?" she asked, throwing away her first line with a suspicion of a wink and a curtsy.

"Look at her!" Annette, with narrowed eyes, nudged the French biographer. "She bows like a chambermaid."

*

It was almost one o'clock in the morning when Wilena Samuels sat down to supper under the Meissen chandelier and lifted a frail squab's thigh between her index finger and her mighty thumb. She helped herself to peas cooked together with young lettuces that held a pearl onion each, imprisoned in their sunless hearts. She realized with the first mouthful of cucumber and watercress salad that while this might be one of her passable suppers, it was not one she would enter in her book under the heading "Triumph," or even "Great Success." (She kept a record of every one of her supper parties, with diagrams of the seating arrangement, comments on the menu, and scraps of witty conversation.) The cucumbers had not been diligently pressed of all their water and, as a result, did not feel thoroughly dead under the tooth. Having marked off her food without any sentimentality, Wilena Samuels turned to the conversation. After a moment, she relinquished her part in the dialogue with the conductor (who broached a happy soliloquy), raised her white-wine glass, and closed her eyes. Inspired, no doubt, by the legend that Caruso's voice had shattered crystal chandeliers, she thought she could tell, with the thin rim of a glass pressed between her teeth, which way the conversation was going.

The impresario, who never spoke, was trying. "Nice dress!" he told Annette.

"I had a sinister quarrel with Balenciaga," answered Annette. "Now I go to Givenchy."

Wilena Samuels lifted the red-wine glass to her lips.

"Ego!" said the French biographer. "In this case Freud slipped! Musicians, today, *have* no ego. They have also lost the art of the grand gesture. Do not forget," he continued with a splendid movement of the right hand, "that 'Litz' engraved *Génie Oblige* on his visiting cards."

To the English comedienne, who was seated next to him,

Guy Dutour said with simplicity, "I know that I have rarely played as well as I did tonight."

"Peroxide and ammonia, followed by sunstroke . . ." Annette indicated her husband's dinner companion to the French biographer; he laughed a quick dry laugh when he noticed how serene Annette's eyes were, and he remembered the words with which he had written them into his fictionalized autobiography: "Ses yeux purs de lapis-lazuli, ses yeux inouïs . . ."

Wilena Samuels once more smelled doom in the air and, intent on dispelling it, rose like a draft from her seat. No one seemed to notice — except the physician, whom she shared with the conductor. He watched her attentively through his bifocals, head lowered and eyes raised, as she walked the length of the table. (Four days ago he'd been summoned to examine her heart, and had charged seventy-five dollars for the house call.)

The English comedienne watched her disappear behind a screen and heard her, beyond the dining room. "I like Wilena," she told Guy Dutour. "But mind you, is she *really* a friend? I mean she's a friend of the Friendly Little Orchestra Association, and she was the best friend the New Friends of Music ever had. She's everybody's friend. And with her zipper fortune, a passion for gros point. You know what I mean — no critical faculties." And she leaned her bare leg, very gently, toward his, until she felt one thinness of wool between the bones of their knees. No response. Very gently, she recovered her leg, took off her rose, and dropped it in his water glass. No response, but then his eyes were absent, his right hand was limp in his lap, and the fingers of his left exercised on the tablecloth.

"Do you know Justin Berg?" he suddenly asked.

＊

Wilena Samuels walked back the length of the table with her caryatid's arms raised high, and in each hand she held a giant bottle opener in the form of a gilded key, which she had purchased at Hammacher Schlemmer's. Upon reaching her seat, she gravely deposited one in front of Guy Dutour, who sat at her right, and one in front of the conductor, who sat at her left.

"Speech! Speech!" lisped the conductor.

Wilena Samuels took Guy Dutour's left hand in her right, and the conductor's right in her left. She was deeply moved.

"You boys hold the keys to my heart," she said. "Yours, tonight, was a triumph! And I feel, in my heart, that Justin Berg, and the other boys, must feel the way we all do here, tonight."

"Bravo!" cried the eminent biographer.

And, gaily, they all scaled the Mont Blanc.

❊

It was a little after nine o'clock, in the white bedroom at the Carlyle, when the ring of the telephone rent Annette's morning sleep; there was hardly any sound at first — just the fleeting vision of a speedboat crossing a lake and fast approaching her shore. Then she stirred in her white satin bed with its headboard in the shape of a shell. (Young and rather perfect, with her pale hair unknotted, she liked, simple-mindedly, to imagine herself rising from it looking like Botticelli's Venus.) She let the telephone ring twice after she removed the Flent from her right ear, and thought, It is Wilena. I must chide her about that blond cliché with the red rose she placed next to Guy last night. No, it *is* Wilena, but it's the critics — it's Justin Berg.

❊

"Hello, my dear!" said Wilena Samuels in her violent contralto. (She had been up since seven o'clock — she had sat on a corner of the Aubusson, in what she called her "nature suit," and done attenuated Yoga; having gone through her mail, she had signed a small check for the Washington Square Music School; she had eaten yogurt, drunk her coffee black, and read the papers — but her real day was just beginning.) "About Justin Berg," she said.

"Yes?" Annette asked, her voice breathy as a child's.

"It's not bad, but his heart isn't in it, except at the beginning." And she quoted the headline — " 'Dutour, the Master, Plays' " — with pride, waited a significant moment, and started on the text: " 'Guy Dutour's rendition of Beethoven's Fourth Piano Concerto — that most mysterious and poetical of the Master's works (which he performed in Carnegie Hall last night) — was skillfully restrained, knowingly conceived, spirited, lofty, and eloquent throughout. The Andante con moto — which has no like in the literature of concertos — was invested with an affecting elegance, at once subtle and meltingly simple, and in the last movement the melodies sang forth.' "

In the second paragraph, Justin Berg had words of praise for the conductor. Annette registered "craft," "insight," "fervent tempi." In the third, he appraised the remainder of the all-Beethoven program; Annette no longer listened. To her, the review given Guy Dutour was a polite, cruel affront. (Yet only two days ago, over dinner at the Pavillon, Justin Berg had seemed as ardent a friend to both of them as ethics allowed. Apparently recovered from his intestinal illness, he had attentively eaten a large meal.) Then she heard Wilena Samuels. "Perhaps I shouldn't tell you, my dear, but it's from the heart. You know that Justin Berg can't get *really* excited about Guy's playing unless it's Liszt or Chopin."

Annette felt her pale cheek struck red by a giant hand.

Wilena Samuels was now proudly quoting from memory: " 'Never before in my entire life have I heard anyone (not even Monsieur Dutour!) give such an unearthly and tonally incandescent rendition of Chopin's E-Minor Concerto. The lyricism he brought to the slow movement was nothing short of miraculous; the moonlit romanza was sung with such feeling and aristocratic address that it evoked in this reviewer's mind visions of the great Polish poet himself, with its melancholy figurations gliding through the air like' — something, something — 'filaments.' "

To Annette, Wilena Samuels' reminder was a direct attack, and the mystery of Justin Berg's inexplicable review was abruptly solved; it had been written — of this she was certain — under an enemy's direct influence. (As indefatigable as a courtier, Annette was the instigator of a thousand and one miniature plots, and suspected everyone else of being exactly like her. Wherever she turned, the horizon appeared hazy with vapors of intrigue, stratagems, conspiracies.) She interrupted Wilena Samuels to ask, "Have you seen Justin Berg since the day before yesterday?"

"Sure. We had dinner that evening, and he had poached eggs with me for lunch yesterday, if you want to call that — "

Annette broke off the connection with a frail, pink-tipped finger, and lay still, the instrument dead on the pillow, next to her ear. It was one of her grave shortcomings in the sphere of musical diplomacy, this lack of control with the telephone. Soon she would have to dial, apologize, blame "the nerves of our North American tour," and invent a new dinner party. She reached toward the night table for Agatha Christie, but her hand, strained in midair, fell back. She felt ferreted out, humiliated, set back in her love for

Guy Dutour. (She might, at times, take a sudden lover, but the nymphlike fidelity with which she labored at her husband's career had always been beyond reproach; inevitably, she had a tendency to praise herself for Guy Dutour's every success — and blame herself for his smallest failure.)

One evening, just about a week before, she had sat on the couch under the Juan Gris and talked so much, and cried so much, late into the night, that Wilena Samuels had ordered her own car to take her back to the hotel, and, on parting, had urged her favorite sedative, like a gift of money, into the palm of Annette's gloved hand; and she had ridden through the dark dawn behind the chauffeur's black shoulders, weeping still, still holding the red and blue capsule tightly inside her black suede fist.

So it was true, thought Annette, that a friend on whom one depends must not be allowed to catch the critical moment . . .

She lifted Agatha Christie from the night table, placed it at the edge of her bed. She would wear the new nasturtium suit from Givenchy under her leopard coat and, hatless, go out in the wind and shoot Justin Berg — twice, somehow — in the pit of his intemperate stomach, then walk east on Fifty-seventh Street and up Fifth Avenue. The elevator man would smile at her; the door of Wilena Samuels' apartment would open. With her face a shiny mask, Wilena Samuels would advance toward her, archaic in long black chiffon and so large a target that she, Annette, with the revolver still warm in her crocodile traveling bag, could not possibly miss the renowned, the generous heart.

Instead, with a frail finger, she pushed Agatha Christie over the edge of the bed, and then she carefully dropped the instrument back into its cradle.

Wilena Samuels sat on the edge of her unmade bed, her

head bowed. Every once in a while she let her chin drop onto her chest. Slowly, she rolled her head toward her left shoulder. Then she rolled it back, very slowly, until she heard several successive, reassuring little snaps. She rolled it toward her right shoulder. Finally, her chin was back on her chest. She repeated the movement clockwise, and heard more muffled snaps. At that moment, Wilena Samuels, who unconsciously gave her emotions a physical form and clothed them in ancient attitudes, looked like an agonizing Amazon. By trying to loosen the tightness at the back of her neck, by concentrating on a specific relaxation exercise, she was trying to forget her heart — her swollen heart, grieved, helpless yet protesting because it had been once more misunderstood; her heart, trying to steal away, its irregular beat suddenly faint, pianissimo. And then again, as she rose to her feet, it fluttered and gave a syncopated jolt. Her physician had told her there was no cause whatever for alarm. She thought of calling him. His diagnostic expositions, and his methods of treatment even more, often verged on the absurd; yet the fundamental insights from which he worked were correct. He knew the round of her afflictions: at least once a day she was struck; more often than not she fell down; always she picked herself up and, totally dedicated, braced herself for her next good deed. But of her rewards he understood very little. For only she could simultaneously walk among her idols and breathe the pure air of her intentions.

As she stood at her bedroom window, a simple addition of reassuring familiarities (sight of the bear cage opposite, in Central Park Zoo, and feel of the worn, thin silk of the carpet under her bare feet) gave her a sudden sense of well-being. Abruptly, she felt restored. She thought of calling Guy Dutour, but there was so little she could say. She sensed that he would never possess the classical repertoire, and the knowledge lay heavy on her heart; besides, an inadvertent word of criticism was enough to make him cancel a concert, several concerts, a tour. And Wilena Samuels never chose to inflict pain of any kind, certain that someone else would come along to do it for her.

She kept the telephone line free. Annette was proud, and would wait a little. But any moment now the lisping conductor, who had trouble getting up in the morning and blamed this on his sinus, would call up and say, "Today the pain is *stupefying!* Half my face, like lead, and then more lead — *bullets* of pain . . ." And after him, the French biographer.

✿

Annette had removed the Flent from her left ear and rung for Gertrude, who immediately brought in yogurt, black coffee, and the morning papers. Gertrude was greatly saddened by Justin Berg's review, which Annette translated for her. They read, translated, and discussed the others. In the repeated laudatory adjectives Annette slowly began to lose Justin Berg.

✿

Annette and Gertrude kept one paper from Guy Dutour. He understood and did not ask for it. Gertrude brought his breakfast into the study, where he invariably slept after a New York concert or recital. He drank a small glass of apricot nectar. Then he ate a crouton of French bread, on which he spread first a thin layer of butter churned in the electric blender and then a layer of the fresh goat cheese Gertrude bought at Fraser Morris'. After hesitating slightly, he ate his croissant dry, and drank a rather large bowl of café au lait. Then he rose from the couch, slid his feet into lees-of-wine gros-point slippers, and, in his pajamas, walked toward the Pleyel. He approached it with all the tenderness he usually reserved for a woman in the morning, if he had ruffled and driven her a bit far in his lovemaking the night before. Malachite settled into a crescent on her cushion by the pedals and panted as she awaited her cue. Guy Dutour started Chopin's platitudinous Nocturne in F Minor, opus 55, no. 1, and played it with such a virgin conception and such tender purity that Malachite fell asleep without a wheeze, and Gertrude, who waited behind the door for the end of a phrase before she could collect the breakfast tray and prepare Malachite for her morning walk, stamped a sneakered foot when she felt the tears come.

The Sin of Pride

DARK, INTRACTABLE, with peeling noses revealing a tender new pink skin underneath, the soles of their feet riddled with splinters, unsupervised, tasting of brine, smelling of slightly scorched skin and stale sun-tan cream, nurtured on white bread, peanut butter, raspberry jam, Fig Newtons, and milk, the children — seven of them — stood on the boardwalk, halfway between the ocean and the bay.

"Let's go to the beach," said Tom, who was twelve and could swim.

"Let's go to the bay," said Tristram, who was small for six, and afraid of the surf.

"I've got a splinter I want to take out," said Tina, who was nine.

"I'll take it out for you," said Tina's twin sister, Tilda. "I know where Mother's hidden the tweezers."

"The sun's right above us — it must be around noon," said Tamara, who owned *The Giant Golden Book of Astronomy.*

Tom looked at her. She was the oldest of the group, and

rather incomprehensible — fourteen at least, and just back from a holiday in Yugoslavia. (Who wanted to go to Yugoslavia, when the island was *right there,* two hours away from the city?) She seemed to be teasing him when she really wasn't. It was her manner, and her English accent. And she was so big (those *shoulders*). And pink polish on her toes — which was all right for mothers, he supposed. And, speaking of mothers, *her* mother kept a shop on the docks (a *boat*ique — yoicks!), which was practical in a way, because Tamara could get a candy necklace for free any time. She usually wore one, and then suddenly, toward the end of the day, she would give it away with a queenly gesture. But the really *good* thing about Tamara was that she shared her raft.

"I think," said Toni, who was Tom's younger sister, "that I should take Thaddeus back to his house." The baby whimpered on the boardwalk, dressed in a tiny cotton shirt and nothing else. "All right, all right, Thaddeus," said Toni, with a penetrating sweetness to her voice, "I'll take you home." Gently, she picked him up and started in the direction of his house.

"It's broiling," said Tamara languorously. "I would love to lie in a hammock, in the shade of two trees."

Tom looked at her. *Two* trees. She probably saw a lot of trees in Yugoslavia. But around here? Bushes, yes; little trees, yes; but for shade she knows perfectly well you have to go home.

"It's Wednesday, isn't it?" asked Tristram.

"Well, I want to go to the beach," said Tom.

"And I want to go to the bay," said Tristram.

"I'm hungry," said Tilda. "And Tina should have that splinter removed."

"All right, then, let's all go home," said Tina, "and go to the beach after lunch."

"But I want to go to the bay," said Tristram.

"Let's all go home," said Tom, "and go to the beach after lunch."

"Where's Theo?" asked Tina.

"Where's Theo?" said Tom.

"Where's Theo?" said Tilda.

"Theo's very handsome, don't you think?" said Tamara.

"I haven't seen my brother all day," Tristram said evenly, although he had most certainly seen him at breakfast.

"Well, as I said," said Tom, "let's all go home."

The children separated into two groups and walked in opposite directions. On the back of Tina's sweatshirt, in bright red, printed letters, it said I'M AN ANGEL. The back of Tilda's shirt read I'M A DEVIL. The children separated again. Tilda went off somewhere with a cat she found under the boardwalk, and Tristram, for no reason at all, ended up with Tina at her house.

*

Flat on his back, eyes blindly closed against the sun, its heat straddling his chest and driving him deeper into the heat of the sand, Theo lay in the sand pit in front of his house. He had come out of the sea shivering only ten minutes ago, but he was beautifully warm now; the summer was his, and he lay there bewildered with joy. This particular summer, he had conquered his very own narrow kingdom by the sea. Infinitely familiar (hadn't he been coming here since he was two?) yet forever renewed ("Tamara, look! They've begun to build the new house! I wonder who'll live in it. I hope it's a really *modern* house!"). This year, the traffic obeyed him; he could stop a beach taxi with a sign of his hand ("Hi, Mr. Thornhill, how's the driving? Found me a turtle yet?"). This year, even Tom obeyed him ("Now, Tom, you let Tina and Tilda have a handicap of three feet; after all, they're *girls*."). He had learned to dive under the surf at last ("Watch me! Here I go! *Watch!*"). On Sunday mornings, he loved to lie on the beach with his eyes puckered, a book carefully placed in his father's shadow, and watch over him ("Toni, take Thaddeus away; can't you see my father's *sleeping?*"). This summer, he had really learned to escape his mother ("Oh, come on, Ma, can't you see I'm busy? Can't you see my friends are *waiting?*"). And he had finished his summer homework and so surpassed Tom, who went to the same school in the city but was a year ahead ("What, you still working on your book report? I've fiinished *mine*").

Theo turned over onto his right side very slowly, observed the sun directly above him through the slit that was his left eye, settled himself on his stomach, decided that it would soon be time for lunch, felt the black heat of the sand pierce his left cheek, raised his head, felt with his hand for an ever so slightly cooler spot until he thought he had found it, moved over slightly, and offered his cheek to the sand once more.

*

The mercury in the deep shade of the living room, climbing in its narrow glass prison and then hesitating and climbing again, by noon had arrived at ninety-six. A moment later, an alarm clock rang in the kitchen, and Theo's mother, who was lowering a tea bag into a teapot and lifting it out, dropped the tea bag, reached for the Baby Ben, stopped the alarm, and wondered, "Where's Theo?"

A sleepy voice answered her through the screen door. "Here, in the sand pit, drying."

Funny, she thought. I spoke aloud. Must be the heat.

"Theo," she said, in a voice that sounded more cajoling

than she intended it to. "Our laundry's on the noon boat. I'll give you a dime if you go get it."

The voice from the sand pit was less sleepy this time, and more assertive. "Tom's mother gives him a quarter when *he* gets the laundry."

"I've already told you I don't care what other people do. I don't think you should be paid a quarter every time you run an errand for me. In fact, I don't think you should be paid at all, but as long as all the other children — "

"I thought you didn't care what other people did."

"Oh, Theo, stop. It's too hot for an argument. Never mind. I'll go down for the laundry myself, after lunch. Where's Tristram? He promised to be home by twelve. Those children."

✻

Those children. Wild, those children with bleached hair. Intractable. Proud. Barefoot, always, with tar under their toenails. Shedding their skin, all summer long. Elusive as lizards. Up and out with the sun, and still out when night fell. This very morning, Theo's mother had seen Tina and Tilda on the boardwalk, carrying an enormous phonograph between them. It was a quarter to seven, and their mother still slept, no doubt. Where were they going with a phonograph at a quarter to seven? Gathering power, those children, from the sun and the sea. Building their sand castles for Thaddeus to destroy. Dreaming. Inaccessible. No need of parents whatever. Never mind the fact that they show no respect and no obedience. Talk to them and half the time they don't bother to answer; they don't even hear you. Ask them to do something and nine times out of ten they don't, because they don't see why they should. Only Toni remained half-tame, sweeping the house in the morning, folding hospital corners on her bed, biting her lip as she wrote down a recipe for home fries. Sweet Toni with the long hair. Warm, dear Toni, whom Thaddeus (who was not, as everyone thought at first, her baby brother) followed on the boardwalk with clucks of joy. But those children, on the whole — the boys especially — tell them to be back at six and they come in triumphant at half-past seven. Give them a watch and they leave it in a drawer. Make them wear it and they forget to wind it. Wind it for them and they forget to look at it. Self-sufficient, that's what they were; their parents could disappear for all the difference it would make, so long as they left them with money for peanut butter. Self-sufficient even on rainy days, they ran from house to house, leaving sweaters and slickers behind. You never knew where you'd find them. The boys at a table, building their airplane models in an atmosphere of silence and male sanctity. The girls on the floor, hectic and high pitched, busy putting together this year's folly — a mouse hotel, with real gingham curtains. ("Well, why *shouldn't* mice stay in hotels?" Toni answered Thaddeus' mother irritably, instead of with her usual temperate sweetness.) And Tom, on one of those rainy days, lost a five-dollar bill his mother had given him to fetch the laundry with. It simply vanished. His mother was very angry with him, but throughout the interrogation Tom remained unmoved. The five-dollar bill had vanished from his pocket. Yes, he had folded it up carefully and placed it at the very bottom of his pocket. From which it had vanished. Magic. ("Gadzooks," said Tom to Theo afterward, "how can I be responsible for a five-dollar bill with legs that *walks* out of my pocket?")

*

"Theo, what would you like for lunch?"

"Peanut butter and jelly on white, ice cream, and mashed banana."

Just as well, thought his mother. It's unbearable to think of putting a match to the stove, except to boil water to make iced tea. Even the morning's wash has me thoroughly depressed.

Theo's trunks, almost dry, were fading in the sun. When the heat of the sand seemed to pierce his eye sockets, he decided, In a moment, I shall have to get up and dip my head in a pail of cold water. Then maybe lunch. I wonder where Tristram is . . . After lunch I'll read, and after that maybe I'll go down to the docks . . . A dime . . . I have seventy-five cents left, as I did not spend my candy allowance. That will make eighty-five cents with the laundry dime. Which means I'll be missing fifteen cents. Tom owes me a dime for the gum he bought for Tamara. I'll ask him for it on my way to the docks, and if I manage to borrow a nickel from Captain Thorpe I can get the Cessna 180. $1.00. I can just make it. There's no city tax.

His eyes still shut, he saw the longish box that contained the Monogram model of the Cessna 180. ("Sport plane. All plastic model scaled from official blueprints. With floats and retractable wheels. Working doors. Engine. Two figures.") One of them was a woman on water skis, who wore a red bathing suit and reminded him of Toni. But then, most women in red bathing suits reminded him of Toni, as most women in yellow bathing suits made him think of Tamara.

Last night, he and Tamara walked back from the docks together. Tamara had gone down to get the laundry off the six o'clock boat, and Theo had met her there by chance. She asked him to take the wagon back to her house. It was heavy with the laundry in it, but Theo didn't want to sound lazy. And as they walked side by side on the boardwalk, Tamara said, above the sound of the wagon, quite loud and with a sidelong glance, "How old did you say you were?"

And he answered, because he *had* to answer, "Ten."

Of course she should have stopped there, but she didn't; she kept right on going. She said, "I'm sure all the girls will be after you when you grow up. When you're eighteen, you'll be a very handsome young man."

He felt embarrassment cloud and mar his face. There was nothing he could say.

"When you're eighteen, you must get in touch with me," she added, vaguely.

"I won't forget," he answered, his eyes on her pink toenails. "I'll pick up the phone and let you know."

Now Theo thought of the laundry and the dime, sat up, then stood up, and, thoroughly dazed, walked into the darkness of his house. "I want lunch," he said.

*

"Let's go to the beach," said Tom.

"I want to go to the bay," said Tristram.

"I'll let you have the raft," said Tamara to Tom.

"I don't need it," said Tom. "Toni's taking care of Thaddeus, so I can take hers."

"It's rough," said Tristram.

"Well, who's forcing you to go in?" said Tamara.

"No one," whispered Tristram.

"Where are Tina and Tilda?" asked Tom.

"They're still up at the house," said Tamara. "They said they'd be over a bit later, with their mother."

"With their *mother?*" said Tom. "What's the matter with them?"

"I don't know," said Tristram. "But I don't want to go in."

"But you don't have to," said Tamara.

"Where's Theo?" said Tom.

"Yes, where's Theo?" repeated Tamara.

"He's gone to get the laundry," said Tristram.

"But is he coming later?" asked Tom.

"Eventually, I suppose," said Tristram, who was learning new words.

Tom took Tamara's raft, Tamara took Tristram by the hand, and the three of them slowly walked down the wooden steps that led to the beach.

"You walk sideways, like a crab," said Tamara to Tristram.

"Ouch!" said Tom as he jumped into the sand. "It's broiling. The sand's much hotter than the boardwalk."

"It *is* broiling," said Tamara with a wilted air. "I can't stand this heat."

"The only thing to do," said Tom, "is to go for a dip."

"Still, I don't want to," said Tristram.

"Run, both of you, run!" said Tom. "And you won't feel the heat of the sand."

*

"Ouch!" said Theo, and he sat down heavily in the middle of the boardwalk. He took his left foot in his hands and bent over it. There it was — a large new splinter had gone straight up the pad of his big toe. Though his preparations had been extensive — he had dunked his head in a pail of cold water, he had counted to thirty before coming up for air, he had put on his afternoon bathing trunks — Theo now wished he had never set out. His bathing trunks had felt cool to the skin, but as soon as he stepped out of the house onto the boardwalk the soles of his feet, although quite tough by now, began to throb with pain, and he knew that even tonight, between cool sheets, he would still feel the heat in them, and that it would be like that time his mother gave him a hot-water bottle and forgot to wrap it in a towel. All he needed was this splinter. Either I go home, he thought, or I go limping to the docks. This splinter needs a needle and tweezers. Incapable of making a decision, he stretched himself out on the boardwalk. "Ouch!" he said again as his naked back came in contact with the burning wood. He got up hurriedly. This is not my day, he told himself slowly, enjoying the statement. He felt dizzy and, as he began to walk again, strangely oppressed. Well, this is something new, he decided. Maybe I'm sick. Maybe it's the heat. I wonder if I'll make it to the docks. I wish there was a cloud in that blue sky. I wish, oh, how I wish . . . oh, I don't know what I wish, but I do wish it would rain.

Careful not to spend his reserves, he hobbled on slowly — right foot, left heel, right foot, left heel. Then he stopped for a rest and closed his eyes. He saw a thousand stars in an orange firmament. He opened them, and blinked against an implacable sun in a shoreless blue sky. It was then that he heard the whippoorwill. That's odd, Theo thought. I've never heard the whippoorwill at this time of day . . . I must rush, because the noon boat will be leaving the docks for the mainland soon, I have a feeling. If I hurry, I can make it, but I really don't feel well . . . Funny about the whippoorwill — he usually sings between eight-thirty and nine. I heard him last night, just as I was going to sleep, and I went to bed at eight-thirty — early, very early, for me.

The whippoorwill sang on, and as he sang Theo heard the distant, faint roar of a motorboat approaching. It was very faint at first, and he wondered who could be arriving in an unscheduled water taxi. Not my father, he thought regretfully; he never comes before Friday . . . And as Theo thought about his father, the sound of the motor grew louder and louder. Theo looked up into the sky but saw no jet, and the roar grew louder still. It was the sound of a motorboat, but amplified, surely. It had grown so loud that Theo's hands came up over his ears, but it was no use; the roar kept on growing until Theo thought the noise would kill him. And at that moment it materialized. Right there, right above Captain Thorpe's house, appeared the head of a being (Oh, no, too horrible . . .) that was unlike any other being — tremendous in size but with only his head showing above the roof of the house. The head obliterated the sun and the sky, and gave off heat. Theo felt hotter than he had ever felt before. The heat came from the being's eyes and mouth, and its ears pointed straight up into the sky. Theo brought his hands to his eyes, but he couldn't erase it; he still saw it, right up above Captain Thorpe's house. He bent in two, thinking that perhaps two thicknesses of him would protect him better than one, and as he did that he lost his balance, tripped, and fell on one knee. Simultaneously, the roar of the motor diminished and died, so abruptly that Theo thought that it was he who had died. But he felt, suddenly, far, far away beyond the beating of his heart, a pulsating pain in his left foot, and he thought, The splinter. I must be alive still; I feel that splinter, far away, in my foot . . . And when he opened his eyes and looked up, he saw the sun and the sky — nothing else. And then he heard the whippoorwill, very faintly. And then he saw Captain Thorpe's house — a white saltbox, with a chimney. And he saw dune grass, and sand, and the ocean. And he couldn't imagine where the whippoorwill was. He couldn't see him, and on that part of the island there was no place for him to be — not a bush, not a tree.

"What's the matter with you, Theo?" asked Tilda.

"Yes, anything wrong?" asked Tina.

The girls stood on the boardwalk with a large phonograph between them and small beads of sweat around their hairlines.

"Let's take him home; he must be sick," said Tilda.

"He looks sick," said Tina. "And he can't even talk. But what about the phonograph?"

"Never mind the phonograph," said Tilda. "We'll just have to carry it over to Theo's house."

"Theo, walk in front," said Tina, who wanted to keep an eye on him.

And so the twins brought Theo home.

*

"I'm cold," said Theo, shivering under his blanket. "Could you make me something hot to drink?"

"I'll make you some lemonade," said his mother, infinitely relieved, as she hurried to the kitchen, because ever since those two girls with their blasted phonograph had brought him home Theo had remained completely silent. She had put him to bed in his bathing trunks, half an hour ago, and watched him, as he lay on his side, drained and pale under the sunburn, and completely silent.

"Also," said Theo, "I have a splinter I'd like you to remove."

She hadn't wanted to ask any questions. The girls said they had found him on the boardwalk, looking "sick and funny." Well, there was nothing surprising about that on such a hot day. She would take his temperature later. Slowly, the water for the lemonade came to a boil.

Theo's heart, as he huddled under his blanket, still beat so violently that for long wild periods he wished it would stop altogether. But he knew that it wouldn't. He tried to decide whether he was better off with his eyes open or shut. He kept them open for a while, trained on Pluff, his brother's stuffed bear. Also, he felt sick — feverish, that is. But it was hard to tell. He often felt feverish; when he had a cold, for example. But then, more often than not, he would be finally, and scientifically, proved wrong. Later this afternoon, much later, he would ask his mother to take his temperature. He felt sick, and yet he didn't. He knew that he would be perfectly well in the morning, if he was ever to be well again.

*

Theo's mother gave Tina and Tilda each a glass of milk and a quarter between them, and asked them to run to the docks and see if they could still get her laundry. There were no sheets left for Tristram's bed. The girls were reluctant to leave the phonograph behind (whose phonograph was it, anyway, and where were they taking it?), but Tilda finally pocketed the quarter, and they left hand in hand. As they opened the screen door, Theo's mother thought they had exchanged sweatshirts, but she wasn't sure. The twins played at being twins, which she didn't like.

*

Where's Theo?" asked Tom, who was digging.

"I don't know. Where's Theo?" said Tamara.

"He's sick," said Tristram, who had been by the house to fetch his shovel.

That seemed to satisfy both Tamara and Tom.

"Is Toni coming?" asked Tom.

"There she is," said Tamara, "coming down the steps. She's got Thaddeus with her, and he's screaming."

"And where are the twins?" asked Tom.

"They've gone to get the laundry for my mother," said Tristram, "and then they're coming down for a swim."

"And their mother?" asked Tamara.

"She's coming, too," added Tristram. "She's still doing her laundry. It's very, very hot, she says."

"Let's all get orange drinks from *her* house and come back to the beach and *then* go for a swim," said Tom.

"I don't know if she'll have that many," said Tristram, who was in a pessimistic mood — something that often happened to him when Theo took to his bed.

"Hello," said Toni, in her new red tank suit. There was a curve to her stomach as she bent down to deposit Thaddeus on the wet sand.

"You're putting on weight," said Tamara.

Thaddeus screamed again.

"Shut up, Thaddeus," said Tom.

❋

Tina, Tilda, Tamara, Toni, and Tom were in the water. "Those children," said their parents all summer long, "*never* come out of the water." They did come out of the water, but only when a grownup went and got them. The scrawny twins, with purple lips and uneven fringes (they were in the habit of cutting each other's hair during the summer months) dripping into their eyes, would shake so violently that they had to be wrapped in towels. Toni and Tom, who had flesh on their bones, usually sat down to rest for a moment, and then, with a new flow of energy they had drawn from goodness knew where, they would begin to build a road, a damp moat, a sandy castle. Tristram never tired of the water, because he never went in. Posed at the very edge, he anticipated each new surge with a loud shriek. But he had learned to time himself as perfectly as a sandpiper; he could run out with the tide, turn around, and run back, and only get the soles of his feet wet. He believed in distant relations with the ocean; they were involved in a battle of wits, not a union. The ocean was getting overfamiliar if it so much as splashed him. One afternoon, it did even more than that. Tristram was building at the water's edge with Tom, Toni, and his brother. He had become so absorbed that he let a wave, unexpectedly more powerful than its predecessors, knock him down. Wet at last, he faced the ocean in a towering rage. "That was unfair!" he screeched.

Tamara swam with long strokes and dived under the water, and then she would walk on her hands. When she did that, only her feet showed, their soles to the sky, ten pink toes facing the water.

＊

The ocean looks big today, thought Tilda — bigger than it has ever looked before. And the undertow is treacherous. Toni had been in trouble a few days ago, and a gentleman who happened to be walking by dived in, and someone then rushed up to Toni's mother's house, and Toni's mother rushed down to the water and dived in, and she and the gentleman brought Toni in by her long brown hair. Toni had been very good, her mother said, and had not panicked, which was the most important thing. But still Tilda had not liked the way Toni looked coming out of the water, with the gentleman bending over her on one side and her mother bending over her on the other side, and Toni gasping a little, her legs under her soft, like noodles, and no color left in her face. That was the worst emergency of the summer, except for that one beautiful calm day — when was it? Oh, a couple of weeks ago, when they brought in that woman who had tried to commit suicide. How she clawed and bit the men who had so kindly brought her in with ropes, and how distressed she looked, all sopping wet, with a skirt and a shirt and all. And the men sort of *threw* her into the police jeep. The crowd was enormous; in fact, practically *everyone* came down, and Tristram, very logical and loud, asked, "Why did she have to get all dressed up to go and commit suicide?" So there had been *two* emergencies over the summer, and Tilda hoped there wouldn't be a third. And just at that moment a wave went over her head. She let go of the raft and went under, but as she came up again the first thing she saw was her mother, sitting at the edge of the water, with a beach towel wrapped around her shoulders, looking straight at her. Tilda gripped the raft. The salt water pricked at her eyes. The water she had swallowed made her burp. Toni laughed; but just then another wave went over their heads. Toni and Tilda managed it, but Tom went under. The children saw him tumble twice underwater. He reappeared at the edge, in the shallow water, where he stood up, facing them and the ocean. He shivered — a long, hard shiver. Then he coughed, and coughed again. Then they saw him count; they saw his mouth moving. Then he dived, and a moment later he was back with them, gripping the raft. After that, Tamara, who was straddling her raft like an amazon, was hit and went under. Tilda went after the raft. Tamara reappeared, gasping, and began to cough. She gulped and choked, and spat and coughed. Then Tina, who had not gone under, who had not swallowed any water, began to cough.

*

Tamara, bent over and dragging her raft behind her, was the first to come out of the water. She did not bother to find her towel but lay down as soon as she reached dry sand. She coughed — a slow, deliberate, deep, hoarse cough, and when her mother first saw her, from the top of the wooden staircase that led to the beach, heaving and lying on her side, she thought, for a short and confused moment, that Tamara had been wounded and was lying there vomiting upon the sand.

Toni was next. She found her towel and fell on her stomach, nose down. She coughed into her towel, slowly, attentively, passively, endlessly. One after the other, the children came out of the sea. They left the rafts by the water, and the rafts moved in and out with the tide. The beach had the disordered look of a battlefield. The children fell where they could. Tom lay in the wet sand at the very edge of the water. Tina and Tilda made their way slowly up the beach, hand in hand but coughing separately, and their mother was so busy observing Tamara and Toni and Tom, and wondering what to do, that she did not get up for them, thinking that they were going home. But when she looked back to check, she saw them, lying in the sand side by side and coughing, and then she saw Tamara's mother coming toward her.

"Oh, if only my nice Dr. Himmel were here!" said Tamara's mother rather hysterically. "I've never seen anything like it."

The mothers stood over their children like conquerors over the slain. Occasionally a mother asked, "Can I take you home?" But the children did not move. Tom asked Tamara's mother to cover him with a towel. He wouldn't budge off the wet sand. Then his mother came down in time to cover Toni. Someone inquired about Tristram; the twins'

mother had seen him run home, coughing, just before
Tamara had come out of the water. And Thaddeus had
been taken back to his house by Toni, when he wouldn't
stop screaming.

*

Theo's mother called the community doctor from Captain
Thorpe's house, because she did not have a telephone. The
doctor had just arrived for a working vacation that would
last a month, and this was his first call. "Don't worry," he
said, "I'll take a jeep and come right over. Too hot to walk,
don't you think? It sure is a hot day. Be there in a few minutes."

Theo had dozed off for a while, but he was afraid of dreaming, so he woke himself up. He was conscious of his mother
sitting at his bedside holding his hand, but he didn't mind.
It was neither here nor there. Why is he letting me hold
his hand without protesting, his mother wondered. For
years he had been reserved and undemonstrative, and she
had respected that reserve. What Theo was conscious of,
what he thought about, was his secret — the fact that he
would never be able to speak, not to anyone, ever, about
what had happened to him. Already he had learned to
live with this knowledge, and was almost resigned to it. But
he wondered why his brother kept looking at him; he wondered if his secret in some way showed on his face. And he
wondered also why Tristram sat cross-legged on his bed,
coughing so intently, with Pluff in his arms.

The doctor arrived, dressed in swimming trunks and
sneakers. He was very tall and very hairy. As he bent
over Theo's bed, his mother noticed that hair grew on the
doctor's shoulder blades and down his back; out of delicacy,
she looked away, and asked Tristram to try and stop coughing.

"And what's wrong with you, my friend?" the doctor asked Tristram. "I thought I had been summoned for your brother!"

He took Theo's temperature.

"The fever is low-grade — just over a hundred. There's nothing to worry about. I'll give him a little penicillin by mouth. He should take it for four days. You can order it from the drugstore on the mainland, and they'll put it on the next boat. The penicillin will prevent complications . . . And don't *you* start anything, young man," he said, and turned menacingly to Tristram. "Well, do let me know; call any time. Nothing to worry about," he repeated as he walked out the door. Tristram started to say something about the fur that grew on the doctor's back but decided against it. His cough bothered him, and left not much will for conversation.

The doctor, walking down the wooden steps to the beach, thought, That child seems to be in a state of slight shock. Sensitive child, probably superior, might grow up into a creative personality. Very impressionable, I'd say. Might have seen something he shouldn't have seen; they often react that way. On the other hand, he could have an infection. It's possible, even likely.

Satisfied, the doctor walked across the sand to where the jeep stood waiting.

❋

By evening, the children coughed less. It didn't happen all of a sudden, but there was an improvement by sundown, and by bedtime they had almost stopped altogether. Tamara's mother had called the doctor about the children's cough. Her voice changed, like an adolescent boy's, from one word to the next. "It's like the plague," she said, "or the floods, or something. They're all doing it — they're coughing their lungs out. What could it be?" And she continued, without waiting for an answer, "It's Biblical, I'm telling you. Maybe the sun won't get up in the morning."

"The extreme concentration of salt in the air," the doctor answered evenly, "on such a hot day might do it. Also, there's a bug going around. Don't worry; they'll all be right as rain in the morning. If there are any further questions, don't hesitate to call."

Now Tamara slept as enchanted girls sleep in fairy tales — flat on her back, head centered on the pillow, one soft hand, a vulnerable child's hand, above her head on the pillow, half-open and palm up. The twins had had a fight about who would sleep in the upper and lower bunks, and they had begun to cough again, but in the end they tossed a coin and climbed into bed. An hour after he went to sleep, Thaddeus woke up coughing a bit. Toni and Tom, who were late risers, still read in their beds. Tom was finishing *Young Thomas Edison*, which was for the overdue book report, and Toni had begun *Doctor No*. Tristram slept. His mother, in the kitchen, softly closed the icebox door and sighed when she saw, for at least the twenty-second time that day, the twins' phonograph on the Formica dining table. Afraid of what he might see, Theo practiced closing his eyes for short periods of time. He remembered a story he had heard, about a little girl who had trouble going to sleep because she had never learned, or nobody had ever told her, or she hadn't discovered, that you must close your eyes in order to *go* to sleep. She would lie there, eyes wide open in the darkness, and wait for sleep as for a visitor who would presently come and shut them for her. Theo was tired. His eyes closed, or else he closed them, and from the depth of that inner, whirlpool landscape that would soon precipitate him into sleep he listened for the whippoorwill.